Collecting a dark curl around her index finger, Blair said, "I've thought about kissing you."

"I thought about you kissing my mouth and my neck and my breasts," Cassie said, her face sliding into Blair's hand.

Blair tried to slow her shallow breathing. "I've thought about you naked."

Cassie rocked back on her heels, calmly undoing her nightshirt.

Blair arrested her hands. The game had gone far enough. "Cassie —"

"I want you to kiss me."

Blair studied Cassie's full mouth. "I'd want more than kisses." Abruptly she released Cassie's hands, rolling onto her back and staring at the ceiling. This was happening way too fast.

Cassie stood. As Blair looked on she pulled her nightshirt over her head. Naked, she said, "Can I get into bed with you?"

With only the barest hesitation, Blair lifted the bedding so that Cassie could slide beneath it.

"I've never done this," Cassie said. "Not with anyone. Not even kissing."

JENNIFER FULTON

THE NAIAD PRESS, INC.
1996

Printed in the United States of America on acid-free paper
First Edition
Second Printing, August 1996

Edited by Christine Cassidy
Cover design by Bonnie Liss (Phoenix Graphics)
Typeset by Sandi Stancil

Library of Congress Cataloging-in-Publication Data

Fulton, Jennifer, 1958 –
    Greener than grass / by Jennifer Fulton.
        p.   cm.
    ISBN 1-56280-092-2
    I. Title.
PS3556.U524G74   1995
813'.54—dc20   94-43989
                                                                    CIP

For my sister Kim,
who knows about loyalty

About the Author

Jennifer Fulton (aka Rose Beecham) is the author of *Passion Bay, Saving Grace* and *True Love*. As Rose Beecham she is the popular author of the Amanda Valentine Mystery Series, *Introducing Amanda Valentine, Second Guess,* and the forthcoming title, *Fair Play*. A New Zealander, Jennifer divides her time between two cities — Wellington, New Zealand, and Melbourne, Australia.

Books by Jennifer Fulton

Passion Bay

Saving Grace

True Love

Greener Than Grass

As "Rose Beecham"

Introducing Amanda Valentine

Second Guess

Fair Play (Fall, 1995)

CHAPTER ONE

How time slinks by, Cassie Jensen thought. One moment you are burrowing into the warm salty nook between your mother's breast and shoulder, the next, you are alone on some street corner in an uncaring city, taxi lights fading in the fog, your possessions in two suitcases at your feet.

It was nearly midnight. The cab driver had set her down just off Brunswick Street, in a neglected pocket of real estate that Melbourne's rapacious developers had somehow overlooked. According to the cross penciled on Cassie's street-map, Aunt Delia's vacant apartment should be right in front of her.

She stared up at a crumbling neo-classical façade sandwiched between a shelled-out church and a warehouse with *24 HOUR TOWAWAY ZONE* painted in luminous green on its doors. Wrought iron grills protected tall sash windows, and an ornamental gaslight illuminated the parquet entrance, casting into romantic gloom a pair of stone lions guarding either side. Someone had woven barbed wire around their pedestals, apparently hoping to deter vandals. Nice neighborhood, Cassie thought.

There were six keys on the spare set Aunt Delia had left with Cassie's mother — the front door, the elevator, the laundry, the mailbox and the two deadbolts that secured the apartment. Pressing the elevator button marked *Penthouse,* Cassie smiled faintly. The word had a sixties ring to it, like *pad,* or *grass,* or *encounter group.*

Aunt Delia had been *hip*. Cassie conjured up an image from her mother's photo albums — a woman in bellbottom jeans and a see-through top, flowers painted on her breasts, eyes weighed down with false lashes and glitter. She had "sat in," Cassie's mother said, meaning anti-war demonstrations.

Currently Aunt Delia was crewing a Greenpeace boat somewhere in the Pacific, on the lookout for Japanese driftnetters. Last year she had placed herself in a dinghy between the Norwegians and a whale, and as a consequence had spent a fortnight in an Oslo prison without a change of underpants. She would never learn, Cassie's mother said.

Normally, when she was not on a protest vessel, Aunt Delia lived an "alternative lifestyle" in a loft on the Lower East Side in Manhattan, with her bisexual husband and his male lover, also Greenpeace eco-troopers. She kept her penthouse in Melbourne so that she would have a base for her occasional visits to Australia.

The stiff deadlocks that secured the apartment eventually succumbed to Cassie's efforts. Pushing her suitcases inside and locking the door behind her, she found the light switch and glanced around. It wasn't so bad; faded denim beanbag chairs, a formica table and orange vinyl swivel seats, purple shag carpet, lava lamps, macramé lightshades.

She investigated the main bedroom. The bed was huge and draped with plush tiger stripe velveteen. At its head was a faux wood grain control panel surrounded by buttoned leather-look burgundy vinyl. No animal products here, Cassie thought, kicking off her shoes and throwing herself into the middle of the bed.

Thankfully it was not too soft. Cassie was used to sleeping on a wooden base at home. She twiddled with the impressive array of switches and knobs on the headboard, finding she could adjust the spotlights on the opposite wall. Another dial activated a CD player that appeared to be a recent addition. There was already a disc in the machine. To Cassie's delight, one of her favorite Patsy Cline tracks filled the room. Sighing, she dimmed the lights, undressed, and climbed beneath the covers, surrendering to exhausted oblivion.

She had no idea how much time had passed or what made her eyes flick open suddenly, but when they did, the room was brightly lit and a figure was standing at the end of the bed.

3

The intruder plucked Cassie's question from her parted lips. "Who the hell are you?"

* * * * *

Blair Carroll was not sure whether to laugh or call the police. The girl in her bed seemed an unlikely cat burglar. Blinking sleep away, she elbowed herself upright, wide blue eyes regarding Blair with fright and confusion. She was just a kid. Sixteen perhaps, her face soft with puppy fat, hair a glossy Irish black, its mop-like style dictated by dense corkscrew curls.

"What are you doing here?" Blair demanded.

The girl wiped her mouth with the back of her hand like a child caught pilfering cookies. For a moment, she seemed on the brink of tears, but summoning an uncertain bravado, she responded. "More to the point, what are *you* doing here?"

"I live here," Blair said softly.

The girl frowned. "You can't. This is Aunt Delia's flat."

Blair was silent, casting her mind back a month to dinner with Delia, Jake and Martin. *Of course, you can stay there. It's just sitting empty.* Delia had insisted. She had a sister, Faith, who lived somewhere in the Australian outback and occasionally used the place. But Faith was a farmer and seldom had the chance to get away. *I'll let her know you're going to be there,* Delia had promised.

Delia had never been much of an organizer, Blair reflected wryly. She was one of those individuals who avoided mundane and unglamorous tasks by assuming

4

someone else would take responsibility for them, which, invariably, they did.

Stifling an impatient sigh, Blair met her visitor's accusing stare. "I think we have a problem," she said.

The sandy-haired woman made them both a cup of hot chocolate. Her name was Blair Carroll and she was a friend of Aunt Delia's from New York. She had won some kind of wildlife film award, which meant she could spend a year overseas researching and filming a documentary on rare animals in captivity. Aunt Delia had offered her the apartment.

Cassie's heart sank. Her plan was ruined. After two years of drought, her mother was considering selling blocks of their farmland to pay for Cassie's studies. But college could wait until the crisis was over, Cassie had decided. She had already ripped up the check her mother had given her for living costs. She was going to get a job and start sending money home like a responsible adult.

Her mother had written to Aunt Delia weeks ago about the apartment. *Delia never gets 'round to replying to letters,* she had told Cassie. *She'll call if there's a problem.*

"Mom wrote," Cassie said. "Maybe Aunt Delia never got the letter."

The American shrugged. "Don't worry about it. I'll find another apartment. There are two bedrooms here, so if you don't mind sharing in the mean-time . . ."

"Of course not." She was being really nice about it, but Cassie could tell she was annoyed. And who could blame her. She was in a foreign country. Her best friend had said she could borrow her apartment. Now she would have to waste time looking for a new place, and then pay rent. "I feel really bad about this . . ." Cassie began.

"Well, don't," Blair responded briskly. "It won't be difficult for me to find a place. This is not New York." Mentally, she walked down 5th Avenue to Central Park, skyscrapers looming. Even in the very center of Melbourne, buildings did not block out the sun.

"Can you see the Statue of Liberty from where you live?" Cassie asked.

Shaking her head, Blair placed her empty coffee mug on the low cane table in front of the sofa. "I'm in the Lower East Side, not far from your aunt. My street is narrow and built up, kind of like some of the streets around here, only the buildings are much taller."

Delia's niece regarded Blair across the brim of her cup with frank curiosity. In Australia, people seemed strangely unfettered by social convention. Staring or smiling at strangers was unlikely to get you shot, Blair supposed, so it was a common pastime.

"Are you homesick?" Cassie asked.

Blair caught a glimpse of herself in gridlock on the Brooklyn Bridge, horns whining, her car rank with exhaust fumes recycled by the air-conditioning. "Not yet," she said.

"I might get homesick," Cassie mused. "I've never

been away by myself like this. I mean, I went to boarding school when I was thirteen, but there were lots of other girls and the teachers. We were never really alone." She glanced at Blair with a trace of hesitance, as though checking for signs of boredom.

She must seem very foreign to a kid who had literally walked off the farm, Blair supposed. It was hard for her to imagine the kind of life Cassie must have led. Sheltered, no doubt. How would she get on in the city? "What are you planning to do here in Melbourne?" she inquired.

"Get a job," Cassie replied. "I'm starting at University next year and I thought I'd earn a bit of money first."

"What kind of work are you looking for?"

"I don't really know. There's lots of tourism here. I thought maybe I could get something in a hotel." Cassie fidgeted with her watch.

Conscious of the time, Blair said, "It's late. I'm sorry I woke you, but I got quite a surprise finding a stranger in my bed." That was an understatement. After a frustrating discussion with a Channel Ten executive whose network already had their "furry friends quota" for next season, she had consoled herself with a late-night double feature at a nearby cinema.

The place had been full of singles sitting a few seats apart. Blair had tried to convince herself that it was better than going to an earlier session, where everyone was in pairs. But with vacant seats on either side, she had felt conspicuous and vulnerable, painfully conscious that she was now alone. Out there. After twenty years. The very last thing she had expected was to arrive home and find that the goddess had sent her some company.

Cassie Jensen yawned and stretched her arms, the thin cotton of her night-shirt revealing a body that was much more womanly than her face. "I'll put my stuff in the other bedroom," she said.

Smart move, Blair thought with a trace of irony. "I'll give you a hand," she offered.

Cassie's brief presence had imbued her bed with the faint fragrance of another woman. The scent unnerved Blair, who was finally getting used to sleeping alone. It was six months since she'd celebrated her twentieth anniversary with Lisa. How could she have known what would happen only weeks later?

Some of her friends had wondered out loud how she could not have guessed. But perception was governed by expectations. Blair had had no reason to be paranoid or suspicious of Lisa's behavior. Lisa was an attorney. Some cases distracted her. That's how it had always been.

Blair searched her memory, as she had a thousand times, for some truth she had resisted seeing. Lisa had spent nights away; she had taken lengthy phone calls; she had lost a little weight. In Blair's mind, it had all added up to a big fat zero. No doubt she had taken refuge in delusion and denial. Her therapist certainly seemed convinced of it.

"Why didn't you tell me you were unhappy?" Blair had asked Lisa the day they formalized their break-up.

"I guess I didn't realize how bad it was," Lisa responded.

"You're telling me you were miserable for twenty years?" Blair could hardly get her mind around it. Had Lisa pretended all along? If so, it had been a convincing façade. "I don't believe you," she said flatly.

"You know I never resolved that stuff with Sue," Lisa said. "I was still in love with her when you and I met. I'd just buried the feelings."

"And now you've exhumed them? Oh, puh-leeze." Blair was incredulous. Sue had been Lisa's first lover, the instigator of a somewhat one-sided relationship based, from what Blair could deduce, on the hero worship of a high school kid for a nineteen-year-old woman of the world. Their love affair had lasted only ten weeks, the exact period Sue needed to kill before starting college.

"I know you're hurt," Lisa said. "This isn't easy for me, either. But I can't live a lie anymore. I'm moving in with her." She expected Blair to hand over half the value of their apartment, half her pension fund, and their car.

"I put you through college," Blair reminded her, stunned, even as she said it, that their twenty-year relationship was being reduced to who had paid for what.

Lisa shrugged. "If that's the way you want to play it . . ."

"I'm not the one who walked out." Even then, Blair didn't believe she'd go. But she did, and four days later her attorneys filed a claim.

Be spiteful, Blair had wanted to tell her own attorneys. *Make her squirm.* Instead she had instructed them to settle. She felt no rage. Only grief.

CHAPTER TWO

Cassie did a slow turn in front of Blair. "Do you think this is okay?" She had chosen her most respectable clothes — a white cotton shirt and pleated tartan skirt. The combination reminded her of her boarding-school uniform, an impression she suspected Blair shared. Staring dubiously at her sturdy, lace-up brogues, she remarked, "Maybe if I had some high heels . . ."

"No." Blair's expression was bland. "I think you look just fine."

Examining herself in the mirrored panels around

11

Aunt Delia's cocktail cabinet, Cassie gave a disgusted sigh. "I *look* about fourteen." She flopped onto a chair. "Well, at least I'll get half fare on the tram."

Blair's mouth twitched slightly. "When's the interview?"

"This afternoon," Cassie plucked miserably at her stockings. "I don't know how I'll ever get used to wearing pantyhose. They feel revolting."

"Maybe you should take one of those kitchen jobs after all," Blair said. "At least you could wear pants."

"The pay is awful. I'd never save a cent." In her first week in Melbourne, Cassie had had two job offers — both of them in hotel kitchens, both of them paying three dollars an hour plus meals. That was something, she supposed. If you could face fried steak and chips after smelling it for eight hours.

"I put myself through college," Blair remarked. "Some friends of my parents owned a delicatessen. I worked there every weekend and all summer during vacations. Even my hair smelled of garlic after a while." She laughed softly.

It suited her, Cassie thought. Normally Blair didn't seem to laugh much. She had one of those squarish, serious faces, her gray eyes often remote, as if her mind were elsewhere. Cassie often found herself wondering what to say when they spent time together. She felt a little in awe of Blair. They had nothing in common. Blair had been all over the world making television documentaries and rubbing shoulders with famous people like Jane Goodall and David Attenborough. What had Cassie ever done?

Blair regarded her with a bright unblinking stare. "Perhaps I'm homesick, after all," she said quietly. "The colors are so different in this part of the world.

I drove out to Hanging Rock not long after I got here. Everything was so red."

"It's the drought," Cassie said. "It's been two years in some areas." She lowered her head. Just thinking about the farm made her feel like crying. Last year they had lost their entire wheat crop and exhausted all their stored feed just to keep their stock alive. They'd had such hopes of spring, but the rains had never come and their pastures were still cracked and barren.

"You must miss your mom," Blair commented.

Cassie gazed out the window, not trusting herself to speak. She yearned for the view from her bedroom at Narrung; a warm breeze stirring the gum trees, the raucous cries of white cockatoos squabbling over the food scraps her mother scattered on the lawns around the homestead.

Blair touched her shoulder lightly. She sounded like an older sister. "You'll be okay, Cassie."

* * * * *

The advertisement had said:

Customer service opportunity for well-spoken young woman. BEAUTIES LIMITED needs a night-shift receptionist with a charming telephone manner. Must enjoy working with other women. Good wages and conditions.

What it had not said was that Beauties Limited, which operated from a pastel-toned office suite on St. Kilda Road, was an escort service.

Its tall, perfumed manager, Antoinette De Ville,

13

said, "We're a high-class agency, Cassie. We arrange everything and accept a fee for the hours involved. Any additional services our ladies choose to provide are entirely up to them."

Prostitutes. Cassie was assailed with mental images of tragic, drug-addicted women in miniskirts and too much make-up. She shook her head, "I don't think —"

Antoinette looked disappointed, her frosted pink mouth drooping in the corners. Uncrossing her long legs and smoothing her tailored skirt across her thighs, she said persuasively, "Lots of girls have applied for this job, Cassie, but you're just what we're looking for. You have such a lovely, cultivated voice. All I want you to do is answer the phone and make bookings."

"Do they come up here . . . the men, er, clients?" Cassie asked.

"Never," Antoinette said. "There'll only be you, and Judy and Nan — the young ladies who do our phone fantasies. You'll have your own office, right next to mine. Come and see." She beckoned Cassie with talon-like lacquered nails.

Cassie peered through the doorway to a spacious office. She could imagine herself working behind the blond oak desk, leaning back in the padded chair with the computer terminal in front of her, making herself delicious cappuccino in the two-cup machine on the sideboard. It was so much more appealing than scrubbing pans in a smoky kitchen.

"Six hundred dollars a week and health insurance," Antoinette murmured. "We look after our staff."

"Why did the other girl leave?" Cassie voiced the question that was on her mind.

"She went back to *work,* once she'd had the baby, dear," Antoinette said, with emphasis on the word *work*. "I suppose with the mortgage and every-thing . . . think about that before you have babies," she recommended in a discreet undertone. "They cost an absolute *fortune.*"

Cassie took a deep breath. "So, she's an escort now?" With a baby to look after. She could almost see the shock on her mother's face.

Antoinette was talking about the job. "So it's Monday to Friday from nine p.m. till five in the morning. If you could start tomorrow . . ."

"I —" Cassie bit her lip. Six hundred dollars. The hours were strange, but all she had to do was answer the phone. "I'm not sure. I mean, I don't have any experience."

"I can see that, dear." Antoinette gave a small throaty laugh. "But I'm sure you'll be a quick learner."

Cassie followed Antoinette into her larger office, her mind in turmoil. Food was cheap in Melbourne. She could survive on sixty dollars a week, plus something for taxi fares, and send the rest home. If she hated the job, she could always leave.

A telephone rang and Antoinette picked it up, saying in her husky drawl, "Beauties Limited. How may we be of service?"

Cassie mentally rehearsed the greeting. It wasn't so very different from *Would you like fries with that, sir?*

Antoinette consulted her computer screen. "Lauren

is available tonight. She's a mature, auburn-haired woman who speaks English, Greek and Japanese. Yes, we take American Express, sir." Replacing the phone in its cradle, she threw a toothy smile at Cassie. "See, it's not so scary, after all."

Cassie tried to smile but her face seemed to be paralyzed. Her mother wouldn't have to know. She could tell a white lie and say she was working in a modeling agency. "I'll do it," she said.

* * * * *

"We should celebrate," Blair said. "How about dinner?'

"In a restaurant?" What could she wear? Cassie wondered. In Melbourne fashionable young women dyed their hair the color of plum sauce and wore black bellbottoms and pale make-up. But Cassie had too much flesh for the vampire look.

Blair raised her eyebrows. "Would you rather do something else?"

Cassie quickly shook her head. Blair would think she was stupid if she admitted she had seldom been out to dinner in her life. The only sit-down restaurants within fifty miles of the farm served pizza.

"I know a place," Blair said. "It's casual, but the food's great."

"Is it expensive?" Cassie felt embarrassed asking. But it would be worse if she couldn't pay her half of the bill.

"It's my treat," Blair said.

"I didn't mean that." At this rate Blair would

wish she had never suggested it, Cassie thought dismally. "I want to pay my way. It's just that . . ."

"Why don't you go and get changed," Blair's voice sounded slightly strained. "We can fight over the check later."

When Cassie emerged from her room, she was wearing loose jeans, neat black lace-up shoes and a rainforest slogan T-shirt Blair guessed was a gift from Delia. She had dragged her dense curls into a stubby topknot secured with a small piece of black ribbon. A faded sweater was knotted around her shoulders.

Feeling a thousand years old, Blair said, "You look great."

"You look nice too. I mean, you always do." Cassie's dark blue eyes mirrored uncertainty.

"I'm glad you think so." Blair dryly acknowledged the awkward compliment. The kid had probably accepted the dinner invitation out of politeness to her aunt's friend, she decided. Cassie seemed unusually tense. Homesick for the outback, Blair guessed, or maybe overcome that she had landed a job and now had to take her place in the real world. "Have you told your mom about the job?" Blair asked.

"Not yet," Cassie replied in a thin, uneven voice. "I'm going home for the weekend at the end of the month. I thought I'd save telling her till then. Keep it a surprise."

Even to an unquestioning ear, the chattered response sounded evasive. With vague uneasiness,

Blair examined Cassie's averted profile. It wasn't possible, she reasoned. Delia's niece was nineteen. Too old to have run away from home, surely. Besides, it was none of Blair's business what the young woman was doing. There was no reason at all why she should feel responsible for her.

Conscious of a sharp surge of relief that they would not be sharing accommodations much longer, Blair checked for her car keys. "Let's go eat," she said.

When Blair asked Cassie whether she wanted red or white wine, Cassie said, "Whatever you like." The only wine she had tasted was champagne on New Year's Eve. At home the farm workers drank ripe dark beer whose musky flavor she did not enjoy.

"So, tell me about the job," Blair asked.

"It's mostly telephone reception — customer services," Cassie parroted the description from the advertisement, relieved she didn't have to lie outright. She could just leave out a thing or two. "The pay is good and the boss seems really nice."

"What kind of business is it?"

Cassie watched the waiter pour red wine into their glasses. "It's a small company in South Melbourne." She summoned all the innocence she could muster. "I'm on the night shift with a couple of other women — starting tomorrow. I can hardly wait."

Blair raised her eyebrows. "Night shift?"

Cassie took a gulp of wine. It dried her mouth instantly, leaving an aftertaste that reminded her of under-ripe plums. Wincing slightly, she licked the residue from her lips. "That's very nice."

Blair couldn't help but smile. She had been *born* older than Cassie Jensen. "I can order a Coke if you'd prefer it."

Cassie shook her head emphatically. "No, the wine is fine."

A young woman wearing tight black shorts with stockings and black shiny boots set down a platter of Mediterranean food between them.

"Mmm, tapenade." Blair tore off some warm pita bread and spread it with black paste.

Cassie followed her example, nibbling the salty combination with an air of distraction.

She was probably looking for a plant to hide it in, Blair thought. Signalling their waitress, she requested a pitcher of water. "Cute, huh?" she observed without thinking.

Cassie stared blankly after the young woman, then returned her attention to Blair, blue eyes innocent of conjecture. She had absolutely no idea, Blair thought. For a moment she contemplated telling her outright *I'm a lesbian.* But what would she gain from coming out to this *child?* She had no idea how Cassie would react, and they had to share an apartment for another week or so. Blair was in no mood to deal with a bout of adolescent homophobia.

Cassie continued to consume her wine as if it were unpleasant medicine. She'd be a heartbreaker one day, Blair thought — as soon as she got some self-confidence. For some reason the idea depressed her. "Do you have a boyfriend, Cassie?" she surprised herself by asking.

Her companion looked amazed. "Me? I hardly

know any guys. We don't exactly have a busy social life on the farm. I mean, we see the neighbors and the farm workers but . . . Anyway, I'm not interested in that kind of stuff." Her cheeks went pink. "Boys 'n everything."

"Sex." Blair said, feeling like a corrupting influence. *Stop teasing her,* she told herself.

"I suppose so. I've never really thought about it." Cassie raised her chin, apparently suspecting Blair of deriving cheap entertainment at her expense. "How about you? Do you have a boyfriend?"

"No," Blair said. "I was with someone for twenty years. We broke up recently."

"Oh." Cassie colored violently. "I'm so sorry. I mean . . ."

Blair was stunned at her searching expression, the welling tears. It was as if Cassie had registered the pain Blair was concealing, and reflected it back at her.

"It's okay," Blair heard herself say. "I'll get over it."

"I only had my father for *fifteen* years, and I'll never be over it." Cassie lowered her head, a stray curl flopping forward.

Blair was silent for a long moment, shamed by the bald honesty of the remark. When had she started inhibiting herself? she wondered. When had sentimentality begun to feel safer than real emotion? She thought about her childhood in safe suburban New Jersey, her teenage years. Nothing had touched her. She was a healthy, happy white teenager with good grades — popular, clever, not so pretty the cheerleaders saw her as competition. Then she had fallen in love with Samantha. They were both fifteen.

It must have been so obvious to the people around them, Blair thought. Within a few months she and Samantha were being ostracized. They had been hurt and bewildered. It was ironic. They had never even kissed.

She met Cassie's gaze. "You're right. I'm not over it. I wish I were."

Cassie's knuckles were white. "You want to wake up and find it never happened. I used to wish I'd never had such a great dad, then it wouldn't hurt so much." Tears plopped off her chin onto her plate. She made no effort to wipe them away.

Feeling at a loss, Blair observed, "Your father must have been quite young when he died."

"It was an accident," Cassie said. "The tractor brakes failed and it went into a ditch. He was crushed to death."

"There's just you and your mom?"

"They wanted more kids, but something went wrong when Mom had me. I came early and they couldn't get to the hospital because there were floods. So Dad delivered me. Then the Flying Doctor came and took us to the hospital in Melbourne."

"The Flying Doctor?"

"That's what we have in the outback," Cassie explained. "Doctors and nurses fly planes to see their patients. It's impossible to drive to some of the stations. It's too far, and there aren't any proper roads."

"Mmmm. The Australian outback reminds me of

Arizona, only it's hotter." Blair tried to imagine Mrs. Jensen, an older version of Cassie, left managing an outback farm and a teenage daughter, while she tried to come to terms with the loss of her husband. "Your mom must have had a hard time."

"Aunt Delia came for a while, when Dad died," Cassie said. "But then she had to leave and stop people killing whales. We're really proud of her. Someone has to stand up for those who can't defend themselves."

You're going to be hurt, Blair thought sadly. *Disillusion will eat away at those bright ideals, and your soft heart will tear and bleed.* She sighed. It happened to everyone. That's what growing up was about — forming enough scar tissue to survive.

Cassie brightened suddenly, "I watched those videos you left by the TV. They're wonderful. I think you're so clever."

"Thank you." Blair felt a flush of pleasure. It was pathetic, she thought, this eternal craving for approval. She invited some more. "Which did you enjoy most?"

"I thought the one about the tigers in India was just fantastic. Is it true that the Indian Government is lying about the numbers to cover up poaching?"

Everyone had asked the same question, especially Delia, who was pressing for a full-scale publicity campaign to expose the aphrodisiac trade that was pushing tigers to the brink of extinction.

"It's impossible to tell exactly how many tigers occupy a large area," Blair said. "But my observations suggest the numbers fall far short of official tallies."

"How can people be so cruel and greedy?" Cassie glowered. "I cried and cried when you showed that dead tiger with her baby licking her."

Blair stared at her food, unprepared to confess the truth, that the shot Cassie had referred to was a calculated piece of propaganda designed to stab the hardened hearts of viewers accustomed to a daily diet of tragedy and despair. Blair had arranged for a game warden to sedate the tigress, whose cub obligingly licked its mother's face then turned to the camera in plaintive protest, its strangled cry frozen on the closing frame, sound dubbed in later.

"What happened to it?" Cassie demanded. "Surely you didn't just leave it there." Apparently interpreting Blair's silence as assent, she cried. "How could you?"

Hastily, Blair said, "The cub is fine. Of course I didn't leave it to die." In fact, it was carefully observed until its mother had regained consciousness and led it away into the jungle.

"Is it in a zoo?" Cassie didn't let up.

"It's in the wild. The wardens on the reserve took care of it," Blair said diplomatically.

This seemed to mollify Cassie. "It's the one thing I hate about farming," she commented. "Breeding animals for slaughter. It seems wrong."

"Are you a vegetarian?" Blair inquired.

"No." Cassie gave a sheepish grimace. "I'm a farmer's daughter. I guess that makes me a hypocrite."

The cute waitress served their meals.

Blair refilled Cassie's empty wine glass, and

watched the waitress saunter away. "We all have our weaknesses," she said, adding silently, *And mine is for nubile young things in tight shorts.*

"Am I drunk?" Cassie stretched her arms high and linked her hands above her head.

Blair fumbled with the apartment key, her attention momentarily riveted on the pull of Cassie's T-shirt across her full breasts. "No, you're just not used to wine."

Cassie went ahead of her, flicking on the lights and collapsing on a beanbag. "I can't move." She yawned. "I'm going to sleep here."

Blair surveyed her flushed cheeks and tangled hair and suppressed an illicit fantasy of Cassie looking equally abandoned, sprawled naked across a bed. "A shower will sober you up," she said, telling herself the same applied to her.

Cassie blinked heavily. Blair's expression was strange, she thought. Kind of distant. Remembering her guarded reference to the loss of her relationship, Cassie felt a rush of renewed empathy for her. "You must be lonely," she said, then frowned. It hadn't come out quite the way she'd intended.

Several feet away, Blair stood quite still, her arms folded. She seemed to have trouble meeting Cassie's eyes.

"I'm sorry," Cassie babbled. "That was so tactless. What I meant was you must miss your boyfriend. I suppose it's like a death in lots of ways. I just wanted to say —" Grabbing handfuls of beanbag, she struggled to get up, but fell back again, releasing a dismayed hiccup.

Blair approached, one hand extended. "I'll run that shower for you," she said unflappably.

Cassie allowed herself to be pulled to her feet. Keeping hold of Blair's arm to steady herself, she apologized again. "I feel for you. I just wanted to tell you."

"I understand." Blair's tone discouraged any further intrusion on her grief.

Impulsively, Cassie planted a small kiss on her cheek. "Thank you for taking me to dinner, Blair."

Blair detached herself gently. "You're very welcome. Congratulations on the job."

The job. Cassie's stomach fluttered. She'd almost forgotten she was going to be working for an escort agency. And a good thing too, or she might have blurted it out to Blair. The last thing she needed was Blair telling Aunt Delia, who would be straight on the phone to Cassie's mother.

Blair was staring at her with searching intensity. Did she suspect her of hiding something? Attempting to sound nonchalant, Cassie said, "Well, I'll take that shower."

"Cassie —" Blair began abruptly, then seemed to change her mind. "It doesn't matter."

"What?" Cassie said.

"It was nothing important." Blair's tone was flat and dismissive. "Go take that shower."

Feeling unsettled for reasons more complex than she could fathom, Cassie retreated to the bathroom. When she had removed all her clothes, she stared at herself in the mirror. Growing up was strange, she thought. Just when you think you know what you look like, something changes.

In her bedroom, with the door closed, Blair listened to the water pipes protesting as Cassie turned off the shower, the soft thud as she climbed out of the tub, faint humming as she dried herself, the faucet running as she cleaned her teeth. Blair could almost see her, firm and smooth as butter, standing at the basin.

Disturbed, but also slightly amused at her lascivious train of thought, Blair waited until the apartment was silent before leaving her room. The sudden return of her libido was something of a surprise. She was not attracted to Cassie, of course. After six months of celibacy, her body had simply woken up.

In the hot blast of the shower, she washed herself attentively, willfully sensual in her soaping and stroking. Her body responded with tingling skin, articulating its craving for touch. The ritual of washing had a nurturing significance for most mammals, Blair reflected. Humans were no exception. To be hot, wet and slippery, skin polished with loofah, brushes or facecloth — the nearest equivalent to a tongue — was comforting and delicious.

In the early years of their relationship, she and Lisa had often bathed together. But by the time Lisa had finished school and gotten her first real job, their habits had altered. The apartment had always seemed full of people, usually members of Blair's creative teams. Lisa would arrive home, fix herself some food and retire to her study. She would often be asleep by the time Blair got to bed.

Their lovemaking had become more erratic over time. They'd talked about that occasionally, concluding theirs was the normal pattern of any long-term relationship. They loved each other. Neither seemed to feel deprived or sexually frustrated. They were comfortable. Secure. Happy. Or so Blair had thought.

Turning off the water, she toweled herself mechanically. She had spent three months in India last year, filming the tiger documentary. Was that when Lisa had started seeing Sue again? When Blair returned, she had seemed strained; too tired to have sex, too busy to have lunch. In hindsight, Blair guessed she had overlooked some very obvious clues. After twenty years, she had taken her lover for granted.

Blair checked the locks, turned out the lights and, avoiding looking at Cassie's door, got into bed. She lay awake in the dark, angry as much at herself as she was at Lisa. Humans are the most curious and complex of animals, she thought, on the one hand, craving love and security, on the other, loathing boredom. In any long-term relationship, it was essential to strike a balance between the two. Somehow, she and Lisa had failed.

What hurt so badly was that in the end Lisa hadn't cared enough to want to save their relationship. Blair had been willing to admit her own failings and to make changes. But she had not been given the chance. Lisa had simply walked out on her.

Blair rolled onto her stomach, hands bunched beneath her pillow. Damn Lisa, she thought. Damn her to hell.

CHAPTER THREE

She would get used to it, Cassie supposed, staring at the computer screen the next afternoon during her training session with Antoinette De Ville.

Details of the escorts were recorded on a database, listed under name, hair color, ethnicity, language and, to Cassie's amazement, breast size. There was another listing called "special", which was, Antoinette said, "For anything a little bit unusual. Some of our clients want their escort to dress in special costumes." She ran the cursor down a checklist that included French maid, nurse, Marilyn

Monroe clone, adding, "The clients pay a little more, of course."

Uneasily, Cassie indicated another menu heading, "What's this?"

"B and D." Antoinette clicked the mouse and a list of terms appeared. "Some of our ladies are willing to escort clients who want to be disciplined." She seemed amused by Cassie's perplexed frown and patted her hand. "Don't worry, dear. Nan and Judy know the ropes, so to speak. If there's anything you're not sure about, they can explain."

Client records were kept in another part of the computer. Some companies did not keep such records, offering their clients anonymity, but Beauties was more concerned about protecting its escorts. Each client had to provide a credit card number when he booked his escort. His card and his driver's license were checked by the escort when she met him.

Antoinette lifted a red cordless phone. "This is our escort hotline. The girls call in when they meet a client, and when they leave him. You take the calls and record them on the computer. If there's any problem, the escort will say 'My next call is at the Paradise Inn.' If that ever happens, your job is to follow the emergency procedure." Antoinette pointed at a notice on the wall.

Cassie's head spun. She felt faint. It wasn't the sweet, overwhelming scent of Antoinette's French perfume, or the thought that within a few hours she would be fixing dates for 'ladies of the night'. It was the sudden shocking sensation that she knew nothing. She had read books and worked long hours on the farm. She had talked about environmental and political issues with Aunt Delia. She watched the news and "Sixty Minutes" on television. But nothing had prepared her for this.

Gazing at the emergency notice, she conjured up a collage of movie images — shadowy figures lurking behind walls, the click of women's high heels, heroes with square chins and guns pointed.

"Don't worry, dear." Antoinette must have sensed her anxiety. "We've never had a real emergency. But a girl has to be prepared."

Cassie told herself she could leave right then. Beauties were paying a lot of money. They had the right to a competent employee. "I don't know how I'll remember everything," she said weakly.

Antoinette seemed unconcerned. "Of course you'll remember. Two weeks and you'll know the cup size of every Beauty on our books!"

"Great." Cassie could almost see her mother's horrified face.

* * * * *

Melbourne Zoo had it all, Blair reflected as she entered the Butterfly House. Acres of land carefully cultivated to replicate a tropical rainforest, hordes of visitors who seemed willing to pay substantial entrance fees, corporate sponsors vying to pay for a new primate facility, and best of all, a highly successful captive breeding program.

The Zoo administrator could not have been more helpful, personally escorting Blair on a tour of the facilities and introducing her to the staff. There would be no problem filming, she was told. Camera

31

crews were a commonplace event. Only a few weeks ago a German production company had been filming in the gorilla enclosure.

In short, the zoo was happy to have the publicity. They might even be able to work something out with a couple of major sponsors . . . a little discreet product placement, perhaps. Assailed with images of orangutans flashing Telecom calling cards, Blair tried to sound excited at the prospect.

The administrator left her at the Butterfly House, with the rejoinder to watch where she walked. A wall of damp heat greeted her, and everywhere she looked butterflies clustered. Flitting drunkenly from plant to plant, seemingly oblivious to the constant popping of flashes and babble of excited voices, they clung to every surface including the bodies of their human visitors.

Blair paused to admire a Blue Emperor that had settled on a feeding tray nearby. It was the size of a small bird, its wings a dazzling iridescent blue, its black velveteen body gently pulsing. How marvelous and elaborate its design was, she thought. It was amazing such a huge insect could keep itself airborne.

She turned at the sound of a child's protests. His mother was attempting to separate his tightly closed fingers. The more she pulled, the tighter he clenched his fist. When he was finally forced to release what he held, a tiny yellow butterfly fell from his hand, its wings crushed. Listening to his mother apologizing to a concerned keeper, Blair thought sadly, nothing ever changes. *Sorry* comes too late.

* * * * *

The apartment was empty when Blair got home. She would see very little of Cassie from now on, she supposed. Their working hours did not coincide and before long Blair would be moving into the apartment she had found that morning.

The place was moderately luxurious — a furnished two-bedroom unit in a large block overlooking the slow-drifting Yarra River. It was a good location, just a few minutes walk from the State Theatre and the Art Museum. She had been lucky to get it. No doubt it helped that the agent had been wildly impressed with her occupation.

Feeling restless, Blair paced into the sitting room and turned on the television. In the week since Cassie arrived the evenings had slipped painlessly by. The young woman was surprisingly easy to be with. They had cooked and chatted companionably. Then Cassie would curl up on a beanbag, her nose in one of Delia's many books, and Blair would sit at the dining table, working on her budget for the zoo documentary.

She guessed that Cassie was making an effort to be unobtrusive. No doubt she would be glad when Blair had gone and she could have the place to herself and play loud rock music, or do whatever it was that nineteen-year-olds did.

Blair stared without interest at the television screen. Men sprawled across one another in an Aussie-style football match. The Australians were obsessed with their brutal national sport, regarding American football as some kind of nancy wimp joke. Australian players wore tiny shorts and no padding of any description. In their confusing version of the

33

game, the action stopped only when someone had to be carried off the field on a stretcher.

Blair had received many culture shocks since arriving in Australia, not the least of which was the realization that many American obsessions were considered bizarre by the laid-back population Downunder. The concept that bearing arms could be upheld as a constitutional "right" was met with incredulity. Why not enshrine the "right" to drink beer, Australian newspapers proposed. Or perhaps as a parallel, the Federal Government could adopt "the Australian's right to barbecue" in recognition of their country's most hallowed institution.

Australia was the same size as the United States, but had a population of only eighteen million people. Like the U.S., it had been settled by migrants from many different cultures, who hoped to make a new life in a land of opportunity. There was an innocent optimism about the place that pained Blair for its stark contrast with the tarnished American dream.

Had she never traveled, she might have imagined no other possibility, she mused, remembering a case study she'd once read. The subject had grown up in an insane asylum. By his standards, craziness was completely normal and fear simply a part of life. He could not imagine any other reality and strongly resisted the idea that any alternative existed. To remain content, it was essential for him to reinforce his own distorted reality, rather than challenge it.

Was that how she and Lisa had lived "happily" for twenty years? Blair wondered. Gloomily, she paced to the windows. She didn't want to start revising her relationship in hindsight. She had loved Lisa, perhaps not with the blinding passion depicted in pulp romances. But theirs had been a comfortable, undramatic love, the kind built on respect, companionship and shared beliefs. The kind that was supposed to last.

Resisting the onset of tears, she stared out across the city. Melbourne was beautiful and very cosmopolitan, well planned and easy to get about in. The people seemed friendly, a response traveling Americans could not always expect. In some countries she had visited, Blair had felt distinctly unwelcome, her presence tolerated only because the greenback held more sway than most of the local gods.

But in Melbourne, Americans were definitely a novelty — and quite a popular one, it seemed. Blair had lost count of the times strangers had helped her and taken an interest in what she was doing. Invariably she was asked if she had been to Ayres Rock, Australia's most famous tourist attraction. It was as if the entire population conspired to keep the north of Australia solvent by sending a steady stream of tourists on a wild goose chase to see a huge rock in the middle of the desert.

Uluru was sacred to the Aboriginal people. "You mustn't take any rock away," Cassie had informed her gravely. "It's very bad luck."

People all over the world were returning souvenir pebbles taken at a time when the sacred significance of the Rock was not respected by white Australians. These pebbles were posted back to Australia by the hundred every month and were sent to the local tribe, who purified them and replaced them carefully at the Rock.

Cassie had sent back a pebble recently, she told Blair, with a letter to the tribe asking them to forgive her for the theft. Blair suspected that she naïvely assumed this would herald a change in the blighted fortunes of her family.

Turning off the television, Blair foraged in the kitchen. On the refrigerator door a note from Cassie with her work phone number written on it. Inside, she had left half a pizza with a second note inviting Blair to eat it.

Perhaps she should get herself a domesticated flatmate, Blair thought. Living with another person had its advantages.

CHAPTER FOUR

Cassie yawned widely. It was four in the morning. Thankfully the phone hadn't rung for nearly half an hour.

"Want some hot chocolate?" Nan, a small woman with very fine spiked blond hair, appeared in the doorway. "Things are slowing down, so Jude and I are taking a break. Why don't you join us?"

"Thanks. I'd love to." Cassie transferred the phones, picked up the cordless hotline and followed Nan across the carpeted hall to an office that resembled a cluttered sitting room.

Stretched out on a frayed sofa, a hefty book face down on her lap, was a woman with shoulder-length brown hair pulled back in a soft ponytail. Adjusting her glasses, she indicated an armchair, and with the kind of distant dreamy expression Cassie associated with poets, spoke into the phone.

"Mmm . . . aah . . . And she's rubbing oil all over my ass. Oh . . . that's so good . . ."

Cassie tried to tune out, but it was almost impossible to ignore Jude's panting monologue. Wishing herself elsewhere, she examined the many posters decorating the walls, recognizing Amelia Earhart, Marilyn Monroe, Martina Navratilova.

Jude finally hung up, rolling her eyes. "Damned diaper fetishists. Only a man who's never had to change one could possibly be turned on." She put a marker in her book and swung her legs to the floor, smiling at Cassie. "How's it going, kiddo?"

"Fine, thank you," Cassie wasn't sure how to describe her first night. She had booked an expensive threesome and a couple of "specials" involving rubber clothing. Antoinette would be pleased.

"You'll get used to it." Nan seemed to read between the lines. "I was on reception before we set up the fantasm line."

Jude opened a packet of chocolate biscuits and offered them to Cassie. "Where are you from, anyway?"

"West of Bendigo," Cassie said, wondering if she had country bumpkin stamped on her forehead.

Jude grinned. "We thought so. You don't look much like a city girl." At Cassie's frowning examination of her attire, she added, "It's not the clothes. I mean you could pass for the western suburbs. It's your face."

Make-up, Cassie thought. As soon as she got her first pay she would buy some pale foundation and dark lipstick so that she could look like everyone else.

"I wish I had your skin," Nan said. "Bloody cigarettes. I look forty."

"How long have you been in town?" Jude asked.

"Only a week."

"Know anyone?"

"Not really. I mean I'm sharing my flat with someone, but she's moving out soon." Cassie caught a look exchanged by the two women but was at a loss to interpret it. "She's a friend of the family," she added, feeling for some strange reason that she needed to explain herself.

Jude sipped her drink. "Where's your flat?"

"Fitzroy," Cassie replied. "It's actually my aunt's place but she doesn't live there, so I'm using it."

"We're in Fitzroy too," Nan said. "On Nicholson Street."

"You live together?"

Nan seemed about to reply when Jude cut smoothly across her. "That's right. We pooled to buy a house."

"We're renovating," Nan added. "One of these days we'll have a floor in every room."

Jude grinned. "And a hot tub in the back yard."

Their banter reminded Cassie of her parents talking about building their swimming pool. Shortly before her father had been killed the foundations and pipes had been laid and a huge number of tiles delivered. They were still in their crates in one of the barns.

A telephone rang.

"It's one of yours," Nan handed the receiver to Cassie.

"Is that you, Bambi honey?" inquired a man.

"Bambi's not here anymore," Cassie said. "But may I tell you about some of our charming and attractive ladies?"

"What's your name, darling?"

Cassie hesitated, her gaze drawn to a poster on the opposite wall. "Cindy," she said, offering a silent apology to the supermodel.

The caller seemed satisfied. "Well then, Cindy. Let me tell you what I want. She has to be blond . . ."

Cassie was surprised to find Blair up when she got home. The sitting room was a sea of camera gear. Figuring Blair was set to start some serious filming, Cassie followed a delicious aroma to the kitchen, where Blair, a striped apron over her usual drill pants and T-shirt, was cooking mushrooms and an omelette.

"Sorry about the mess. I'm shooting without a crew at the moment." She indicated the food. "Want some breakfast? There's plenty for two."

Cassie responded with enthusiasm. "I'm starved. Is there anything I can do?"

"You can make the coffee and set the table," Blair said. "How was work?"

"Busy," Cassie said.

"You weren't by yourself all night, were you?"

"Oh no. There's Nan and Jude. They're really nice." Cassie measured coffee grounds into the plunger.

"What exactly does your company do?" Blair asked.

Cassie had prepared herself for this question. Reciting the story she had dreamed up during the slow periods, she said, "It's an urgent placement service. If a client needs someone, they phone up and I make the arrangements." Detecting slight puzzlement in Blair's expression, she added with conviction, "We have staff on standby all the time. I sent out two nurses tonight."

Blair carried their food to the table. "I'm glad you got home before I left. I have some good news."

Cassie savored her first mouthful of mushrooms, then said, "What's that?"

"I found an apartment."

Cassie stopped chewing. She felt slightly thrown by the news, a reaction that puzzled her. It was not as if it were unexpected. Trying for enthusiasm, she said, "Great. Where is it?"

"Southgate. By the Yarra River. The present tenant is leaving in a fortnight, so if you can put up with me until then . . ."

"It's fine with me," Cassie assured her, aware of a hollow feeling in her stomach. "I mean, I like having company. It's kind of spooky with the church ruins next door and the cemetery out the back."

Blair broke open a crusty bread roll. "Perhaps you should consider getting a permanent flatmate."

Cassie gave a noncommittal shrug. "I'll see how it

goes." She wondered if Blair was annoyed. They had never discussed the possibility of extending their *ad hoc* arrangement. Cassie had figured Blair would raise it if she was interested.

It had crossed her mind once or twice that Blair might have wanted to bring a man home. She was in her late thirties, after all. It must be terrible having to start over, when you thought you'd found the person you'd spend your life with. She didn't seem desperate. But it was hard to tell. At any rate, sharing an apartment would cramp Blair's style, Cassie felt certain.

"Oh, by the way." Blair slapped her forehead lightly. "I nearly forgot. Your mom called last night. I think she was kind of surprised to hear me."

Cassie almost choked on her food. "What did you tell her?"

"I introduced myself," Blair's tone conveyed a hint of reprimand.

Rebuking herself for sounding accusing, Cassie flushed slightly. "Er . . . how is she?"

"She seemed just fine," Blair replied. "I suggested she call again this morning."

Conscious of Blair's level stare, Cassie kept her eyes firmly fixed on her plate. "Did you mention my job?" she asked politely.

"No. I said you were well. She's looking forward to your visit at the end of the month."

Cassie forced down another mouthful of omelette. The delicious breakfast seemed to have lost all its flavor. She hated lying. It was bad enough telling fibs to a stranger like Blair, without deceiving her mother as well.

"Cassie," Blair continued in a neutral tone. "Is there something you'd like to discuss with me?"

Cassie felt her chest constrict. "No." Even to her own ears, her voice sounded remote. Avoiding Blair's eyes, she made a show of buttering another piece of toast. Blair couldn't possibly know about Beauties, she convinced herself. And even if she did, it was no skin off her nose. Blair had plenty to do without worrying about what her friend's niece got up to. Besides, Cassie was an adult. She could do exactly as she pleased.

Out of the corner of her eye, she watched Blair get up and carry her dishes out. A moment later she returned and began packing her camera gear into a series of cases.

"How long have you been doing this?" Cassie asked.

"Making documentaries?" Blair stood upright, absently rubbing her left shoulder. It was an old injury, she'd told Cassie. She'd fallen off a camel in the Indian desert. "I started when I was thirteen. My Dad bought me a Kodak eight-millimeter movie camera." She laughed. "Those were the days when everyone made home movies — *Mom, Dad and the kids at the Grand Canyon . . . Betty Jean's Graduation.* My first movie was *Our Dog Rusty.* I spent weeks training him to jump through a hoop, then he wouldn't do it."

"That's so typical," Cassie grinned. "My dad's old dog Cassius Clay used to do tricks. Dad even taught him to stand on his hind legs with a pair of boxing gloves on his front paws." She fell silent, embarrassed to admit to something which was likely to be interpreted as animal abuse by a wildlife expert like Blair. "Dad really loved Cassius," she added hastily. "I mean —"

"Amazing isn't it, the silliness animals will tolerate from the people they love?" Blair said gently.

"I think humans are like that too," Cassie said. "We put up with a lot when we love someone." She thought about her mother and made a silent promise to make up for her complaints about having to help out on the farm.

Blair was staring, her gray eyes serious and shadowed. "Sometimes I wonder if it's worth it," she said.

"Love, you mean?"

Blair shifted her attention to the begonia plant on the window ledge. "I was with my partner for twenty years. I made a lot of sacrifices. I grew up believing you reap what you sow, but now I'm not so sure."

"Neither am I," Cassie said. "My mom has poured everything into the farm. She's hardly had a life since Dad died. And for what? Flies and dust and dead sheep. It's not fair."

"Is that why you came to Melbourne, Cassie? To get away from it?"

"I can never get away from it." Even as she voiced the thought, Cassie could see herself at a pavement cafe wearing fashionable clothes and make-up and drinking cappuccino with a group of trendy people who wore small round sunglasses. She would still check under the table for snakes.

Aware of Blair's silent regard, she got up and stacked her dishes, then headed for the door.

"Cassie." Blair's voice arrested her. "Are you doing anything on Sunday?"

Cassie turned slowly, balancing the plates. "It's my day off."

"I know. I wondered if you'd like to come out with me. I'll be filming at Werribee, the open range zoo."

Cassie hesitated, wondering if Blair had invited her only out of a sense of moral obligation. Perhaps she felt beholden over the apartment. "Won't I be in the way?"

"I could do with some help, actually." Blair's tone was matter of fact. "This stuff weighs a ton and I don't have an assistant yet."

Cassie brightened. "Well, I'm pretty strong," she said, comforted that she would have a role to play. "And I'd love to see the park."

Blair threw her a casual smile. "It's a date then."

The telephone rang as Cassie was climbing into bed. Chewing on her lip, she let it ring a couple of times while she rehearsed her story. Then she snatched it up.

Her mother sounded tired. She had been out on the western boundaries for a couple of days, she explained to Cassie, shooting starving sheep. "There's no choice," she said without emotion. "It would be much crueller to leave them."

"Well, don't kill any more. Please." Cassie begged. "Bring them into the southern paddocks and buy some extra feed."

"I can't." Her mother sounded utterly defeated.

"You can. I've got some good news," Cassie was aware she was babbling, but she felt a surging desperation. Her mother needed her and she was not there. "Listen to me, Mom. That check you gave me. I don't need it. I've got a job."

"What do you mean, you've got a job?"

"I work nights so they're paying me extra. I'm going to send you money — hundreds of dollars every week."

"Oh, Cassie —"

"It doesn't matter about college. There'll be plenty of time for that when things get better."

Her mother was silent. Cassie could almost hear her thoughts. *You know how important your education was to your father. The world is a much bigger place than Bendigo.*

"Mom," Cassie said. "You've done it all, ever since Dad died. It's my turn now."

"I know you want to help, darling," her mother said huskily. "But we've lost sixty percent of our stock. Most of the lambs are dead. We have no grazing pasture at all and it's already summer. I can only pay wages for a few more months. To be honest, I'm about ready to walk off the land."

"No!" Cassie cried. "Please. I'll think of something, I promise."

"I'm so tired, Cassie."

"I know." Mentally floundering for some ray of hope to offer, Cassie said, "You have to trust me, Mom. We're going to be okay. Now, listen. Get Stan to drive the rest of the stock into the Southern paddocks. Use my college money to buy some extra feed. I'm coming home in a week. We'll talk then. And don't kill any more sheep, okay?"

"Okay." She could hear her mother blowing her nose. "I'll make myself a cup of tea and pull myself together. I wish you didn't have to think about all this, Cassie. I feel as if I've let you down."

"Well you haven't." Cassie wiped her eyes. "You're the best mother in the world."

Her mother laughed softly. "Perhaps that's because I'm the luckiest."

A little later Cassie lay awake listening to the daytime bustle of traffic beyond her window and thinking about the farm. If only they could discover oil like the "Beverly Hillbillies" or invent some kind of rain machine.

What was wrong with the world? Floods in one part, drought in another. The Antarctic was melting beneath a huge hole in the ozone layer, dead volcanoes were coming to life, tigers could be extinct in fifty years. Aunt Delia was right. The party was over, and no one was prepared to clean up the debris.

Cassie closed her eyes and imagined clouds assembling over Bendigo, bruised and heavy. Thunder rolling. The miracle of rain.

CHAPTER FIVE

"This place is fantastic," Cassie said, clinging to the handgrip as Blair steered their jeep toward a belt of gum trees. "It's wonderful to see the animals out there roaming around."

Blair smiled at Cassie's enthusiasm. The young woman was surprisingly good company, intelligent in her observations and uncomplaining in her assistance. Filming animals was an exacting task. They were never there when you wanted them. A low plane was bound to fly over when you were poised to capture significant behaviors. There was always some loose cannon whose antics would throw a placid herd into panic, especially when you had finally inched your way close enough to get some decent footage.

Filming in a zoo like Werribee had definite advantages. The animals were confined to large open enclosures which could easily pass as the wild. They were well fed and relaxed, and were unfazed by jeeps full of inquisitive humans. Their behavioral repertoires were largely maintained, thanks to the zoo's careful attention to environmental factors.

"This is very similar to San Diego," Blair observed. "They divided their collection into a confined exhibit zoo and an open range park like this. It works very well."

"What's your new documentary about?"

Good question, Blair thought. In her mind it had started out as a feature on unusual captive breeding environments around the world. She had envisaged Singapore Zoo with its commitment to natural barriers only, its night-time safaris, and its theories about educating visitors by allowing very close proximity to animals. And there was Melbourne, with its remarkable rainforest environment; Jersey, where Gerald Durrell bred less glamorous gravely endangered species, and had animals sharing their enclosures with one another. San Diego had a brilliant frozen embryo and test tube program . . . the material was endless.

"To be honest, I haven't quite settled on my subject," she admitted. "It started out as a kind of 'zoo as ark' feature, but that angle has been pretty well covered. Anyway, it kind of bothers me that if zoos are presented as the safety net for species survival, people will be let off the hook — they can relax about conservation because someone else is doing it."

"I think you underestimate people," Cassie said. "It's such a huge problem, no one knows where to start. But it's not that we don't want to help."

"I wish I could share your faith in humanity," Blair said. "In my experience people don't want to hear how bad it is because it challenges them to do something."

"You sound like Aunt Delia."

Blair gave a small involuntary smile. "Your aunt would not agree. Delia thinks I make chocolate box crowd-pleasers."

"Do you?"

"I'm guilty of wanting my work to sell, like any other filmmaker." Blair swung sharply on the wheel to bypass a huge pothole in the dirt track. With an apologetic glance at Cassie, she asked, "You okay?"

"That was nothing," Cassie assured her. "I'm used to the outback."

Blair drew to a halt beneath a stand of gum trees. In the distance she could make out a pride of lions. "Let's have lunch here," she suggested. "We can shoot those lions in the afternoon."

Cassie stood on her seat, binoculars trained on the big cats. "There's a baby." She gasped. "It's just gorgeous. And five or six lionesses. I can't see any males."

"They're probably asleep under a tree," Blair said dryly. "It's something our two species have in common. The females do most of the work and the males make most of the noise."

Cassie flopped down in her seat. "Do you think you'll get married again, Blair?" she asked carefully.

Slightly flummoxed, Blair said, "I'm planning to stay single for the moment." She should tell Cassie the truth, she thought. But she had already decided to wait until she had moved to the new apartment. There was no reason to compromise their harmonious and undemanding cohabitation.

Contrite blue eyes regarded her. "I'm sorry," Cassie said. "Sometimes I put my foot right in it. It's just that I think you should be prepared to give it a second chance. I mean, just because it didn't work out the first time doesn't mean it's all over forever."

Amused and touched at her young companion's determination to rescue her from her cynical self, Blair said, "I may fall in love again. I'm not ruling it out. But next time I'll think very carefully about the kind of relationship I want."

Cassie nodded. "You've got your own career. I guess a lot of men are threatened by your success."

Not just men. Blair took a bite of her bread roll. Had Lisa felt threatened? She was a competitive person, perhaps even more so than Blair. Had she resented the attention Blair was getting at a time when her own career had reached an unspectacular zenith?

"You'll find it doesn't take much to threaten men, Cassie. They're used to having everything their own way, and they seem to think women should support them in this. God forbid we might have our own goals."

Cassie spread soft cheese on a cracker. "You don't have kids?"

Blair shook her head, thankful that was one complication she had managed to avoid. Several years back, Lisa had started talking about having a baby, but they'd abandoned the idea, unable to see how the demands of child-rearing would fit in with their careers.

Taking off her hat, she fanned herself slowly, enjoying the scent of eucalyptus in the hot dry air. It was good to get out of the city. At one time, she had found it difficult to imagine surviving without an urban infrastructure. Her first overseas trip had been a rude awakening.

Experimenting with the idea of making a travel documentary, she had found herself marooned in northern Thailand without toothpaste, Tylenol, bathroom tissue or, worst of all, insect repellent. Somehow it had never occurred to her that she would not find a 7-Eleven or its equivalent every few miles. It was a wonder she hadn't contracted malaria. Nowadays, she would think twice before venturing into the tropics again. Thanks to world-wide misuse of antibiotics, mosquitoes now carried a deadly drug-resistant strain of the malaria virus.

Blair allowed herself to gaze at the young woman beside her, taking pleasure in the outline of her breasts beneath her flimsy T-shirt, her strong solid thighs, her rosy cheeks and full mouth.

Cassie looked up with an engaging, guileless smile, which slipped abruptly into wavering uncertainty, as though something in Blair's expression had disconcerted her. Running the back of her hand over her mouth in a small unconscious gesture of confusion, she glanced away, then almost immediately returned her attention to Blair's face, as if seeking reassurance.

Blair wanted to find an inconsequential smile, but

as her mouth parted, she found she needed to catch her breath. In vivid, shocking detail, she saw herself kissing Cassie, sliding her fingers into the soft luxuriance of her curls, licking the dewy perspiration from her throat. Her mouth dried and her nipples hardened.

"Is something wrong, Blair?" Cassie asked hesitantly.

Conscious of the color that had flooded her cheeks, Blair expelled an uneven breath. "Nothing's wrong." *Except that I would dearly love to remove your clothing.*

The situation had its irony, she reflected. She had often made contemptuous remarks about men's much vaunted mid-life crisis. Now, here she was lusting after someone barely twenty years old.

No doubt attributing Blair's awkwardness to the stress of her recent break-up, Cassie seemed to shrug it off. Pouring a tumbler of Coke, she asked, "Would you like some?"

"Sure. Thanks." Blair cleared her throat and told herself to get real. Cassie was Delia's niece, completely off-limits. Besides, there was nothing to suggest that the flare of attraction was mutual. Blair was well aware Cassie viewed her as the older generation. And the twenty years between them was probably the least of their differences.

Her ego, Blair reasoned, had suffered a severe blow. It was only natural that she would be attracted to someone like Cassie Jensen: young, impressionable, inexperienced, probably straight — in all, as safe a lust object as she was likely to find. So long as she kept a lid on it, the revival of her libido was probably a good thing. Sooner or later she would find an appropriate outlet. Meantime, there was always her vibrator.

Tipping the rest of her Coke onto the dusty road, Blair started the engine. "Let's go check out that lion cub."

It was dark when they got home. Relieved she did not have to go to work, Cassie scraped the remains of their picnic lunch into the trash and washed the dishes. Blair had gone back down to the car to collect the rest of her camera gear. She would soon have a crew to take over the technical logistics, she'd told Cassie. She was negotiating with one of the television networks. Depending on the deal struck, she might use their staff or employ a crew of her own.

She must be famous in America, Cassie thought. Or at least well known in her field. Cassie wished she could think of someone to impress with the information that she had been out all day filming wild animals with a celebrity. She resisted the impulse to ring her mother, guilty somehow that she had spent the day enjoying herself when her mother was breaking her heart over the farm.

She could always ring the girls on the neighboring farm. But somehow she doubted the Murphy sisters, whose main ambition was to marry the snake farmer down the road, would be interested.

Conscious of a movement in the doorway, she glanced around to find Blair propped against the jamb, rolling a cigarette.

"Oh," Cassie murmured, a little startled.

Unexpected heat flooded her cheeks. "You gave me a fright."

"I'm sorry."

Blair was studying her with the same intensity that had unnerved Cassie earlier that day. Covering her self-consciousness with a small laugh, she said, "It's okay. I didn't know you smoked."

"It's just an occasional vice. Don't worry. I'll hang my head out the window." Blair remained slouched against the jamb, the unlit cigarette cupped in one hand, the other absently soothing her shoulder.

Unsure what was expected of her, Cassie doggedly wiped the dishes. "I had a wonderful time today. Thank you."

Blair gave a slightly wry smile. "You were a great help." She seemed to grow more irritated with her shoulder, shrugging it with a grimace of pain.

"That shoulder is really bugging you, isn't it?"

"It gets stiff when I've been carrying a camera all day."

"I could rub it for you," Cassie offered impulsively. "I'm quite good."

"It's okay," Blair said. "I'll take a pain killer."

Cassie could understand her reluctance. There was nothing worse than entrusting a sensitive spot to an amateur, only to find yourself unable to move afterwards. "Mom has back problems," she explained, by way of reassurance. "So I went to massage classes in Daylesford during the vacation last year. I've done Swedish and shiatzu."

Blair moved out of her casual stance and into the kitchen. She was slightly taller than Cassie, a difference more noticeable as she drew closer. Strands of gray filtered through the sandy brown hair she

55

brushed back from her forehead. Fine lines encircled her eyes, adding humor to the sharp intelligence of her gaze.

"Well, I'm impressed," she said. "To be honest, I could really use a massage." She picked up a terry towel, instructing Cassie. "Leave those dishes. I'll dry them."

"What about your cigarette?"

Blair shrugged. "I think it's the idea I find most satisfying. I gave up years ago but every now and then I get a craving, so I take a few puffs, and it tastes disgusting." Her expression was comical.

Grinning, Cassie wiped her hands dry. "It'll probably be easiest if we use your bed."

"My bed?" Blair's expression seemed to freeze.

"I'd rather you were lying down," Cassie explained. "I'll have to do your back first to relax all your muscles."

"Sure. Fine." Blair started toweling dishes. Her nonchalance seemed forced.

Guessing she was trying to be brave about her pain, Cassie said sympathetically, "We can stop if it gets too much for you."

"My thoughts exactly," Blair said.

"Tell me about your mother." Blair asked as Cassie methodically kneaded oil into her back a half an hour later.

"Her name is Faith," Cassie said. "She's quite a lot older than Aunt Delia. She was born in Sydney during the war. Her dad went to fight in Egypt. She says she didn't know who he was when he came back home. Strange, isn't it, Australians fighting in Egypt, with the Japanese on our doorstep?"

Blair mumbled something, transfixed by the delicious pressure of Cassie's thumbs on the base of her spine.

"Mom's great." Cassie went on. "I know you're supposed to fight with your parents, but she's my best friend. I don't get on that well with girls my own age. Mom says I spend too much time with older people, like her."

"I think that's typical for only children." Blair said.

"Do you have brothers and sisters?"

"Two brothers, both younger. Elliot got married recently, and Greg is a divorce attorney in L.A. We've never been close. I've often wished I had a sister."

"What about your parents? Do you get on?"

Several answers came automatically to mind. 'No', or 'only when I'm not there' were the most honest. But Blair was loath to sound so dismissive, in the face of Cassie's obvious yearning for her father. "We have our differences," she said. "Mom and Dad are very conservative."

"They must be proud of you."

Blair concentrated on the feel of Cassie's hands, rhythmically easing the tension that had built over the past few months. Her parents had been proud of her at one time, she recalled, when they believed Lisa was just her roommate and one happy day she'd arrive home with a man, preferably a doctor, and a ring on her finger.

She winced as Cassie explored a particularly tender spot. "I guess I should have seen my chiropractor a while ago."

"I'll say." Cassie probed the rigid tendons and knotted muscles. "Your back is out of alignment, probably because you're over-compensating with your good shoulder. I'll bet you're getting headaches, too."

"You sound like my mother," Blair remarked.

"No," Cassie corrected pertly. "I sound like *my* mother."

"Your mother turns into a tyrant when she gets someone at her mercy?"

Cassie laughed. "No. But I do." She administered a series of small slaps which made Blair's skin tingle. "Just because you have a broken relationship doesn't mean you have to punish yourself. I can give you some relief, but you have to listen to your body. Stop taking those pills and start being kinder to yourself."

"Hey, enough already." Blair attempted to turn her head in protest, only to find herself pressed firmly down, Cassie's thumbs locked onto an excruciating stress point.

Very close to her ear, a voice said sweetly, "I have to do this, I'm sorry. Just breathe through the pain."

Cassie left Blair sleeping. Sitting on the sofa, she picked up a book that was lying face down on the coffee table. According to the jacket, it was the story of a white woman who had gone walkabout with an Aboriginal tribe. The sheer unlikelihood of the premise made her flick through the pages, imagining with some amusement what Aunt Delia would say.

She got very indignant about the appropriation of indigenous culture and spirituality, especially when it made money for white people.

All the same it was amazing glimpsing her country through the eyes of an outsider who clearly knew nothing at all about the culture or people she was attempting to interpret. Did Blair also find Australia bizarre? Cassie wondered.

She thought about America, as she understood it from school and television — a big dangerous place where people carried guns as if it were a normal thing to do and milk cartons were printed with pictures of missing children instead of cows.

Aunt Delia said that was just one view and when Cassie finished college she must come and stay in New York for a while. You can't judge the world by what you see on television, Cassie's mother often said. For a start you'd have to accept that women only make up about twenty percent of the population.

Cassie closed the book and blinked wearily. She missed her mother.

CHAPTER SIX

Blair pressed the button for the sixth floor and hoped she'd brought everything with her.

Dean Wiebusch, the man she was meeting, was a newly appointed programming executive with the ABC network, which had already aired several of her documentaries. The network was Australia's largest, its programming mix designed to appeal to a broad audience, with particular emphasis on educated middle-class Australia.

After putting feelers out to the various channels, Blair had decided to propose a joint production deal with ABC. The network had welcomed her initial approach and she had followed this with a formal proposal. Today she would talk them through the details and, hopefully, arrive at a verbal agreement.

Blair gave her name at reception and stood in the waiting area admiring a painting.

"Blair?" A chunky blond man strode toward her.

As Blair turned, his expression altered from urbane smiling welcome to puzzlement. He directed a faint scowl at the twitchy young receptionist. "Where did you say Mr. Carroll was waiting?"

Blair took a pace forward and, offering a diplomatic smile, introduced herself.

Dean Wiebusch shook her hand. "I am sorry, *Ms.* Carroll." Again he scowled at the receptionist, as though she were somehow to blame for the assumptions he'd made about Blair's gender.

Blair kept her face carefully blank. Delia had warned her about Australia's extremely sexist culture, but it was still shocking to witness such an unprofessional display of male petulance.

Dean Wiebusch led the way to a meeting room that looked like a hangover from eighties corporate excess. Everything was leather, chrome and smoked glass. A series of abstract paintings occupied the available wall space, chosen no doubt to match the power furniture.

Apparently unaware of the negative first impression he'd made, Wiebusch took on the role of suave host. "Care for a drink?"

"Not for me, thanks." Blair removed her proposal document from her satchel.

"You don't mind if I do?" Wiebusch was already pouring bourbon over ice.

Blair could not help wondering how many times a day he indulged. The guy looked flabby and out of condition, a state that seemed typical of white-collar Australian males, as far as Blair could discern. By contrast, Melbourne seemed to have more than its quota of anorexic-looking women. This had struck Blair as an interesting visual commentary on the state of gender relations.

"So, er, how long have you been in the business, Blair?" Dean licked brandy off his lips.

"Nearly twenty years," Blair replied. "I started my own production company eight years ago."

"And since then you've done pretty well, huh?" He flicked through his own set of papers, pausing to comment on the awards and nominations she had received. "Impressive."

Blair sensed a hint of dubiousness. "Well, it's nice to please the critics," she commented dryly. "But I'm more interested in the viewers. I understand my documentaries have rated well for the ABC."

"Looks that way, doesn't it?" Dean Wiebusch uncapped a fat Mont Blanc fountain pen. "And your new project makes a lot of sense to the network. We want in."

This time there was no mistaking it — the unspoken "but".

"Of course we'll need to talk through the fundamentals," he went on. "The network has a few concerns."

"Such as?"

"Well, before we sign on the dotted line, we have to be certain that you have the resources and expertise to guarantee the outcome."

"I feel exactly the same way," Blair said coolly. She had taken an unaccountable dislike to Dean Wiebusch, she realized. And she had the distinct impression the antagonism was mutual.

"Then you'll understand our position," Dean continued in a self-important tone. "We've never worked with you. On paper your credentials stack up. But you're asking us to commit serious money —"

"I'm not sure if I'm reading this right, Dean." Blair cut across him. "But you don't seem confident I can make a documentary. My work was good enough for your network to purchase and screen during peak viewing hours. I'm not sure what evidence you require beyond this —"

Dean Wiebusch raised his hands in mock defense. "Now don't go jumping to any conclusions. The network is very happy with what we've seen. We just need to iron out a thing or two. Now, I was thinking . . . on the production side, I'd like to see you working with one of our top guys, Mark Antonopolous."

"Excuse me?" Blair examined her proposal, wondering if she had not stated clearly enough that she would select her own team, with the possible exception of the technical crew.

Wiebusch was scribbling on a notepad. "You'll like Mark," he assured her. "All the ladies do. So . . . it looks like this . . ." He pushed the sheet toward her. It listed Mark, the ladies man, as executive producer and had Blair down as sharing producer and director credits with him.

Blair almost laughed out loud. "I think there's been a misunderstanding," she said firmly. "I'm not looking for someone to take over my production. I've approached your network as a possible co-production partner. That's all."

"And we're happy to run with that," Wiebusch assured her. "But as I said, we need to feel confident. I'll talk this over with programming. I'm sure we can make Mark available . . ."

I'm not hearing this, Blair thought. She was being treated like some kind of beginner, incapable of making a documentary by herself. No one had suggested an active role for the network during her preliminary discussions. She hazarded a guess that Dean Wiebusch, the new kid on the block, had arrived at that conclusion on his own.

Compressing her lips, Blair stood and gathered up her papers. Wiebusch looked faintly startled as she extended her hand. "I won't take any more of your time, Dean," she said, telling herself to keep her cool. One executive with an attitude problem was no reason to burn her bridges with the entire network. "Thanks for meeting with me. I hope we can resolve this and do business."

Wiebusch got to his feet, his heavy brow clouded. "Uh . . . right. I'll talk to Mark."

He didn't get it, Blair thought as she descended in the elevator. She had told him in words of one syllable that he could stick his idea, but he hadn't got the message.

She was still fuming when she got home. It did nothing for her temper to be greeted with a wall of noise. Cassie appeared to have unearthed Delia's record collection. The Rolling Stones were complaining at full volume that they could get no satisfaction.

You too, huh? Blair thought, pulling the plug.

Into the merciful silence, Cassie protested. "Hey . . ." She appeared in her bedroom doorway, hair wrapped in a towel, her face covered in some pale make-up. She was wearing only a bra and panties. "Oh, it's you . . ."

"You were expecting someone else?"

Cassie colored beneath the artificial pallor. "I was just playing some music while I get ready for work." She advanced into the room, apparently unconcerned about her semi-clad state. With an indignant look at Blair, she turned the stereo on again, this time lowering the volume to one of background noise. "Don't you like the Rolling Stones? I thought you would. I mean, they're from your era."

"So was Nixon, and he left me cold," Blair retorted.

Cassie faced her, hands on hips, in a distracting display of flesh. "Gee, what's eating you," she demanded.

Blair all but rolled her eyes at the choice of words. Forcing her gaze away from the smooth length of Cassie's thighs, she said succinctly, "I just didn't feel like listening to that sexist shit. I've had enough for one day."

Cassie's mouth formed a small round *oh*. With the air of a reasonable person humoring a maniac, she took the Stones off the turntable, and brandishing a Joni Mitchell album, asked, "Is this downbeat enough for you?"

Jolted by her poise, Blair murmured, "It's fine."

Cassie surveyed her unflinchingly. "Just because you've had a lousy day, you don't have to take it out on me." Without another word, she stalked off to her bedroom and slammed the door.

What a perfect end to a perfect day, Blair thought. Giving way to a juvenile impulse, she turned the music right up, grabbed her satchel and headed for her own room.

Half an hour dragged by before there was a knock at her door and Cassie poked her head in. "Shall I play the other side?" she inquired sweetly.

Blair hurled a pillow at her, thinking even as she did so, *Terrific, now I'm entering my second childhood.* To her complete surprise, Cassie responded by catching it, then heading toward her, eyes sparkling with wicked challenge.

Blair could only resist temptation for a moment. Grabbing a pillow of her own she anticipated Cassie's first feint and caught her a sound thwack around the middle.

Before long they were pillow-fighting like kids, Cassie scrambling across the bed when her pillow was eventually whipped out of her hands.

"Oh no, you don't," Blair scrambled after her, preventing her from reaching it. Tiny feathers spiralled down on them as they wrestled for control of the remaining pillow. In the end, panting and laughing, Blair managed to straddle Cassie and pin her shoulders down.

"I win," she shouted, tossing her pillow aside and making victory signs.

"You cheated!" Cassie cried.

Bending very close to her, Blair said softly, "I won fair and square because I'm older and smarter."

She could feel Cassie's rapid breathing and smell her mild floral scent. The young woman was gazing up at her, the freshly applied eye shadow and plum-colored lipstick making her seem older, no doubt the desired effect. Cassie's mouth was slightly parted, revealing front teeth that overlapped a little from what might have been childhood thumb-sucking.

They would kiss now, Blair thought, if this was the movies. And Cassie would sigh and link her hands behind Blair's neck. Uncontrollable passion would overtake them. They would tear off the shackles of conservatism and, of course, their clothes.

Blair stared down at Cassie, who stared right back. A more realistic alternative presented itself to Blair. The kiss, then Cassie bursts into tears and slaps her face. Promptly loosening her grip and moving aside, she allowed Cassie to sit up.

Dusting herself off, Cassie said brightly, "Want to go out for burger?"

Yes, ma'am, romance was definitely off the menu. "Sure," Blair said, picking tiny feathers off herself.

Doing the same, Cassie remarked, "That was fun. I wish . . ." She frowned.

"You wish what?" Blair asked.

"I wish I was twenty-five. Then I'd know everything and I wouldn't feel so —"

"Young?" Blair offered dryly.

"Dumb," Cassie corrected.

They got off the bed, flicking away the last of the

feathers. Glancing around the room, Cassie said, "I guess it was real groovy back in the old days. Does it make you nostalgic, Blair?"

The air of contrived innocence was so blatant Blair knew she was being baited. "Why, you cheeky brat." She followed Cassie along the hallway, administering a swift, teasing slap to her rear.

To her complete shock, Cassie glanced over her shoulder with an exaggerated flutter. "Mmmm, a spanking," she simpered. "I can hardly wait."

CHAPTER SEVEN

Antoinette had already gone when Cassie arrived for work. She often did that, diverting her phone to Nan and Jude, as if they didn't have enough to do on the fantasm line.

Flicking on her office light and stashing her carry-all in a desk drawer, Cassie went along the hallway to let the other women know she had arrived. The sight that greeted her from their open doorway made her halt, transfixed. Nan was sitting in Jude's lap. They were locked in a passionate kiss.

Cassie's first instinct was to flee but she felt

completely paralyzed, barely able to breathe, let alone move. Her mind seemed sluggishly unable to process what she was seeing. Two women kissing.

Abruptly she remembered the giggling speculation in her high school class over Miss Ross, a teacher who wore masculine clothing and no make-up. Liking the teacher in question, Cassie had always felt shamed by her own nervous complicity in the tittering groups.

She wet her lips, wanting desperately to be able to say a loud casual "Hi" and walk in as if nothing were happening. Instead she opened her mouth and released a gasp that had curdled somewhere between her gut and her throat.

Nan lifted her spiky blond head. "Oh, Cassie. G'day." She seemed completely untroubled.

Jude was more reserved, soft brown eyes combing Cassie's face with quizzical intensity. "Are you okay?" she said, easing Nan out of her lap.

Before Cassie could prevent herself, she gave voice to the obvious. "You're lesbians."

"I'm sorry we didn't tell you before." Jude's tone was soothing. "We thought you had enough to deal with getting used to this place.

Cassie's gaze shifted to the phones lined up along the desk. One was ringing. Nan picked it up and carried it to the far side of the room.

Jude got up. "Come in and have a cup of tea, Cassie. We can take your calls in here for a few more minutes." She filled the kettle from the tap and placed teabags into three cups.

Cassie watched her closely, seeking hints of her sexuality. She didn't look at all like Miss Ross.

Admittedly the teacher conformed to the kind of stereotype insecure people pointed to as a measure of their own supposed "normality."

How ridiculous it was, Cassie thought, to be shocked by a simple kiss. She had seen thousands of clinches on television. She had read the steamy bits from dozens of the Murphy sisters' Harlequin romances. And here she was working in an escort agency, for goodness sakes. At Beauties, she had learned more about human sexual behavior in a week than she had in the past nineteen years.

Meeting her eyes, Jude said. "I'll bet you don't see too many dykes around Bendigo, huh?"

Dykes. Cassie remembered her mother telling Aunt Delia off for using that word. It was no longer an insult, Aunt Delia said. And she should know, she had even been on gay rights marches with her bisexual husband. "We don't see much that's interesting in Bendigo," she responded in a low voice.

"Tell me about it," Nan returned the phone to the desk, muttering about two-minute wonders. "Small towns. They give me the shits."

"She's from Wangaratta," Jude explained.

"And still recovering," Nan added. "Got out when I was fifteen."

"You ran away?" Cassie asked.

"Sure did." Nan sounded pleased with herself. "Came to Melbourne. Got a job in a milkbar, scooping ice cream. That's how I met my first girlfriend. She was the owner."

"She loves to tell this story," Jude intervened, lifting one of the phones and passing it to Cassie.

The caller didn't seem to know what he wanted.

The Beauties sounded too short, too tall, too smart. In the end he decided they were too expensive and he would go to another agency.

Cassie thanked him for calling and dropped the phone in its cradle, muttering, "Buy yourself a blow-up doll, why don't you?" Amused at her companions' startled expressions, she informed them brassily, "I'm not Pollyanna, you know."

Jude lifted an eyebrow with the amused indulgence that seemed the province of people over thirty. Her expression reminded Cassie of Blair in one of her superior moods. "Did you have any idea about us?" she asked.

Cassie shook her head. "I never thought about it. I thought you were just friends sharing a house."

"Like you and the woman you share with?" Jude asked.

Cassie hesitated, uncertain quite how to qualify her relationship with Blair. They didn't know each other well enough to be described as friends. "Blair's not exactly a flatmate. She's a friend of my Aunt Delia, who owns the apartment. She's just staying there for a week or two until she moves into her own place."

"Then you'll be on your own?" Nan asked.

"I thought I'd see how it goes," Cassie responded. "If I get lonely, I'll look for a flatmate."

"Let us know," Jude said. "We might be able to help."

"Thanks." Cassie felt a pang of guilt at her immediate assumption that any friend of Nan's and Jude's would be a lesbian, as if that was a problem.

Apparently detecting her misgivings, Jude said mildly, "We don't bite, Cassie. And it's not contagious."

Feeling color flood her face, Cassie said, "I guess you'll find this hard to believe, but it's not a problem for me. It's just a shock. I feel like some kind of idiot. I mean, it's obvious, isn't it. This place..." She gestured at the posters on the walls. "Martina Navratilova, k.d. lang —"

"Lesbian hall of fame," Jude commented.

"And that photo of the march. I never realized what those signs said. Queer Pride," she recited. "Gay Rights Now."

"That was the big Stonewall Twenty-five March in New York," Nan said. "A million people. It was fan-bloody-tastic."

Cassie tried to comprehend the entire population of her home district a thousand times over. "All gay people?"

"We're not such a rarity," Jude said. "Although as soon as the media gets involved, its the incredible shrinking queer syndrome. They can't stand to report real numbers. In fact, it's a wonder they report us at all."

"So much for their platitudes about the public's right to know," Nan said.

"They're the worst censors of all." Cassie recalled many dinnertime conversations with her mother and Aunt Delia. "Censorship by omission. They choose what we get to hear about."

"Look at the Sydney Gay and Lesbian Mardi Gras," Jude said. "It's the biggest in the world and it's been going for nearly fifteen years. But they never reported it on television until last year." She paused to take a phone call.

"We go every year," Nan said. "I love the parade, but the crowds are hard to handle. It used to be only queers but now mobs of straight people turn up as well."

"Surely that's a good thing," Cassie said. "I mean, if they support it . . ."

"I used to think that," Nan said. "But a lot of them are just there to perv. They're really homophobic. It makes me angry, I guess, because it's so damn typical. They don't know how to party, so they crash ours. Can you imagine how they'd behave if the situation was reversed?"

Cassie thought about Miss Ross walking through the courtyard during recess, groups of girls staring after her, hysterical giggling erupting the moment she'd vanished inside a building. Those kids became adults. Did their attitudes change that much? "People can be very cruel," she said.

Jude finished her call and smiled at her companions. "What's happening here? Queer politics — a crash course for beginners?" Reaching for Nan's hand, she said, "Do you know any lesbians, Cassie?"

"I'm supposed to say some of my best friends are gay, right?"

They broke into laughter.

"You seem okay about us," Jude remarked, as if the idea were novel. "Are you?"

Cassie felt confounded. "I suppose I am. I mean, it's not as if you're serial killers, or something. Anyway, it seems completely natural that you two would be a couple." She caught a glance the two women exchanged. "See. It's so obvious. I must have been blind."

Several phones burst into shrill life. Rolling her eyes, Jude observed, "It's those damned ads Antoinette put in *The Herald Sun*. Shoe fetish fantasies a specialty. News to me."

The apartment was silent, Blair's presence evident only in the few dishes draining on the kitchen bench, the lingering traces of the fragrance she wore, the extra towel in the bathroom.

Cassie washed her face and briefly contemplated the showerbox. Although Blair had insisted the rattling pipes did not wake her, Cassie always felt guilty taking the chance. This morning she doubted she could get to sleep anyway. Her mind felt like a traffic island, the events of the evening endlessly circling.

She paused in the hallway outside Blair's bedroom and stared at the door. It was slightly ajar. Tentatively Cassie nudged it wider, her gaze fastening on the inert lump on the bed. Blair didn't move, and taking tiny steps, Cassie approached her.

She was sleeping on her back, arms flung outward as though she had fallen from a height and now lay unconscious in the exact position she had landed. Guiltily, Cassie regarded her. How would she explain herself if Blair woke? What was she doing in here anyway? Curiosity? Insecurity?

Cassie often used to creep into her mother's room to watch her sleep, taking comfort in the rise and fall of her chest, the faint flush in her cheeks, the flicker of her eyelids. This ritual had its roots in her father's death, she felt certain. She had simply needed to check that her mother was still there.

She gazed down at Blair. In sleep, her face was smooth, the small furrow in her brow softer. A few strands of hair clung to her damp forehead. Her mouth was slightly open, her breathing soft and regular. Up close, her eyelashes were dense and straight.

You never really get the chance to look at someone unless they're asleep, Cassie thought. She liked the shape of Blair's mouth with its slightly roguish pucker in each corner. Heat seeped into her cheeks as she caught a mental flash of Nan and Jude kissing. Blair stirred. For a moment it seemed she was going to wake, but she rolled onto her side, murmuring something unintelligible.

Seizing her chance, Cassie crept from the room. She would make herself a cup of hot chocolate and read a book, she decided. And, very much later, after Blair had gone to work, she would go shopping for some Melbourne essentials. Sunglasses. Platform shoes. And a flimsy sunfrock. If only she were a stone lighter, she thought gloomily. No one made clothes for a thirty-eight-inch bust.

Blair woke late. She had forgotten to set the alarm, or was there some Freudian explanation? The last thing she felt like today was another meeting with another television executive.

After her abortive discussion with Dean Wiebusch, she had called another contact at the ABC who had arranged an off-the-record meeting, in the guise of lunch, to talk about the project. Blair wondered if it was worth bothering with the hassles of co-production. She had calculated that she could finance the project herself if she trimmed the overhead back and spoke very nicely to her bank manager.

But technical production was always the worst headache for independents. She could always try one of the smaller commercial networks, but no one could match the post-production muscle of the ABC. Just thinking about their facilities made Blair drool. She wanted that deal, but not if it meant surrendering control of her project.

Rubbing the sleep from her eyes, she pulled on a robe and headed for the bathroom, hoping the shower wouldn't wake Cassie. Like many of the buildings in this part of Melbourne, the apartment block dated back to the turn of the century, when it had served as offices. Sometime in the sixties it must have been converted to residential units, with the exception of the plumbing, which behaved as if it were a hundred years old.

Standing beneath the erratic hot water jet, Blair soaped herself absently. She would be moving out in ten days, to a luxurious modern apartment in a high-security block. By Melbourne standards, it was expensive. But by the time the currency translated, it cost a third of anything comparable back home.

For a moment, Blair contemplated asking Cassie if she'd like to share. There would be plenty of room, and it was much more comfortable than Delia's place. But the rent would be a hurdle, she figured. Cassie Jensen was very stubborn about paying her way.

Blair's thoughts strayed to the previous evening. Something about Cassie's behavior nagged at her, a vampishness that seemed completely at odds with her inexperience. Toweling herself, Blair was conscious of a hollowing in her stomach. For all that Cassie's mock flirtatiousness was obviously a parody, it had revealed a woman rapidly throwing off a sheltered girlhood. Blair found that woman very attractive.

You would never meet a Cassie in New York, she thought. Kids of twelve had sharper edges, and by nineteen it seemed to her that most young women could barely distinguish their emotions from the armor of cynicism that disguised them.

Blair dressed with her usual brisk efficiency, observing as she did so the looseness of her clothing. She had lost some weight since she broke up with Lisa, the outcome of a diminished appetite combined with a frantic work schedule. Under stress, it was her habit to neglect herself. She hadn't had a haircut for several months, she realized. The results framed her face more softly than her usual minimalist trim. She quite liked the difference.

Turning in front of the mirror, she checked out the rest of her shape. Not bad for a woman disappointed in love. It was lucky, she supposed, that she was not the kind of person who comforted herself with chocolate and fried chicken. Life was stressful enough without having to buy a whole new wardrobe a couple of sizes up.

Applying her customary dab of perfume, she

sauntered into the sitting room, stopping short as a dark head lifted from the arm of the sofa.

Cassie blinked up at her. She looked chagrined. "Oh, I must have gone to sleep. I was going to go shopping and have a rest later."

"You look exhausted," Blair said. "What do they do to you in that place?"

Cassie gave a half-laugh, displaying her usual reticence about discussing her job. Blair wondered if she felt self-conscious. She was aware that Cassie was somewhat in awe of her, probably imagining documentary-making to be much more glamorous than it was.

"I'd better go and get some sleep," Cassie said. "I'm still not used to working at night."

"What do the other women do?" Blair asked. "Surely there's not enough demand for emergency care to keep three of you occupied answering the phone."

Cassie's eyes seemed drawn to the floor. "It's amazing what people want."

"I suppose there's quite a lot of administrative work."

Cassie nodded. "We have a computer system. When a client calls, you have to enter all the information."

She didn't sound particularly enthusiastic. Perhaps working in the real world was not as exciting as she'd expected. "Are you enjoying it?" Blair asked.

Cassie raised her head. "In some ways. I like the women I'm working with, and the boss is nice. I . . ." She chewed on her lip.

Guessing at the reason for her awkwardness, Blair

said, "You haven't told your mom what you're doing, have you?"

"Only part of the story," Cassie admitted. "Things are pretty hard at the moment. On the farm."

"Because of the drought?" Television coverage had shown convoys of emergency supply trucks headed for the drought areas.

"We could have survived for two seasons, but this will be the third," Cassie said. "I don't know how Mom's going to cope."

"Do you feel guilty about leaving?"

"Yes, and I miss her. But there was no point in staying. At least if I'm earning, I can contribute something."

Blair couldn't imagine that Cassie's modest wage was going to make much difference to a bankrupt farm, but she could understand her need to feel she was helping out. "You're visiting your mom this weekend aren't you?" she asked.

"On Sunday." Cassie sighed. "I'm only going to get a day and a half. I don't have to be back until Tuesday night, but the bus leaves in the morning. I'd hire a car, but I don't have my license yet. I mean, I can drive, but it was only around the farm and out in the country, so . . ." She shot a transparently hopeful glance at Blair, then frowned as though annoyed at herself.

Second-guessing her, Blair said. "I'd be happy to drive you, Cassie. I would have offered sooner, but I figured you probably had your own plans."

Cassie brightened instantly. "No . . . I mean, I'd love you to, if you want to. I mean, it's not the best time to see the farm, but I could show you around."

"I wouldn't want to impose," Blair said hastily.

80

"I'm sure your mother has enough to do." Cassie had obviously decided she was inviting herself for the weekend. It hadn't been her intention, but the idea certainly had some appeal. She'd never ventured into the outback. This would be the perfect opportunity.

"Mom loves to have visitors. I can call her now." Cassie gave Blair's arm an impulsive squeeze. "I'm so glad you're coming," she enthused. "I wanted to ask you, but I thought you'd be bored."

"Me being such a city girl n'all?" Blair put in dryly.

Cassie tilted her head to one side, her eyes playful. "Me being such a country bumpkin, more like."

CHAPTER EIGHT

The wooden sign swinging above a pair of weathered gates read NARRUNG.

"It's an Aboriginal word for moon," Cassie said.

Sun might have been more apt, Blair thought, glancing up at the sky. As Cassie jumped out to open the gates, a rush of hot air entered the jeep, accompanied by the usual complement of opportunist flies. Like moisture-seeking missiles, a couple of these immediately zeroed in on Blair's mouth.

Brushing them aside, she passed through the gates and waited for Cassie to rejoin her. The dirt road they bounced along was pitted with holes and forked continually between stands of river red gums. Cassie could have navigated it in her sleep, Blair guessed, swinging the wheel in response to the young woman's directions.

Cassie was flushed with excitement, her feet shuffling impatiently. "Toot the horn," she instructed, as they crossed onto a dry creek bed bordered by scruffy mallee trees.

Blair could see no evidence of a house, but obligingly sounded the horn. Negotiating an uneasy path around clusters of cannonball-sized boulders, she was thankful she had invested in a Toyota Landcruiser rather than the hatchback the salesman had wanted to sell her.

They left the riverbed and climbed steeply along a minor ravine, dust rising in their wake. Ahead, Blair could make out a clearing beneath some spindly eucalyptus trees.

"We're nearly there," Cassie said. "Toot again."

As they reached the hollow, she touched Blair's forearm. "Will you stop? Just for a moment."

"Here?" Blair applied the brakes. The shady spot was well above the surrounding country, no doubt providing a view of their surroundings.

Cassie got out, almost before Blair had switched off the motor. Heading for a stony outcrop, she signalled Blair to follow, yelling as an afterthought, "Don't worry about snakes. They sleep in the heat of the day."

Very sensible, Blair thought, pulling on her wide-brimmed drill hat and scaling the rocks to stand a few paces below Cassie.

"There." The young woman swept an arm over a

landscape Blair might have expected of a Western movie. Only instead of sage and mesquite, the arid land was dotted with distressed-looking mallee scrub. In the distance, the horizon was a reddish brown, pockmarked with gray where vegetation was still clinging to life.

"Normally it's all in wheat over there," Cassie indicated the plains that stretched to the West. Offering her hand to Blair, she added, "C'mon up here. You can see the farmhouse."

"It's like an island," Blair observed, comparing the pocket of green to the surrounding brown.

"Mom loves her garden," Cassie said. "It used to be bigger, but we can't spare the water."

Blair shifted her gaze to Cassie's face and gave her shoulders a gentle squeeze. "C'mon. She'll be waiting for you."

The woman who descended the veranda to greet them was nothing like Blair had imagined. Faith Jensen was tall and deeply tanned, with graying blond hair tied back in a ponytail. Any resemblance she bore to her sister Delia was fleeting. Possibly the mouth, Blair decided. Full and faintly puckered in each corner. Cassie's was the same, but clearly her black hair and pale complexion had come from her father.

Hugging her daughter with one arm, Faith introduced herself and extended a hand to Blair, saying in her broad Australian accent, "Welcome to Narrung. Come inside, both of you. No point in standing out here feeding the bities."

The house was a rambling wooden structure skirted by deep verandas which overlooked lawns and flowerbeds that were obviously cherished. A flock of large white cockatoos swooped overhead as Blair unloaded luggage from the jeep.

It was a relatively common sight in the State of Victoria, where numerous varieties of parrots occupied urban and rural areas. All the same, Blair still could not get used to seeing what was considered a rare cagebird flying by the hundreds. "They're incredible," she said.

"There's a lot of wildlife hanging around," Faith observed, lifting a couple of Blair's camera cases. "They come for the water."

"Did you shift those sheep?" Cassie asked, following her mother indoors.

"Yes, Cassie. And we got lucky." Faith placed the cases inside a doorway, informing Blair, "That's your room." Returning her attention to her daughter, she said. "Three weeks worth of free feed from the emergency convoy. I could have kissed their tires."

"That's fantastic." Cassie hugged her mother. "See. I told you everything would get better as soon as I sent that rock back to Uluru."

Blair met Faith's eyes and saw past the cheerful welcome to a deep despair. Faith Jensen was on the verge of a breakdown, she suspected. The latticework of lines that etched her face spoke of profound physical and mental exhaustion.

"I'm glad you're here," Faith said. "Delia has told me all about you."

* * * * *

What did that mean? Blair wondered as she changed into shorts and a singlet top. Had Delia told her sister that Blair was a lesbian? It seemed likely. Blair was aware that the bond between the sisters was very strong, despite their geographic separation. Faith, it seemed, had taken up the role of mother to the much younger Delia when their own had died.

Blair felt quite certain, Faith did not seem to be the kind of woman who would discuss someone else's private life behind their back. Slightly disconcerted by her instant warming to Cassie's mother, Blair set about unpacking. It was not like her to judge anyone by first appearances. She had never been a person who made snap decisions about anything. Blair felt most comfortable with a situation when she could take the time to measure it carefully.

The decision to tell Cassie about her sexuality was a case in point. Blair felt she had learned enough about Cassie to predict how she might react. Timing was now the issue.

It struck Blair that this weekend might be the perfect opportunity. Cassie was in her own environment. She had her mother there to talk to. There was no way she could feel compromised. And if she did, Blair was moving out in a week. In the meantime, she could always stay in a hotel.

Blair located the guest bathroom and washed her face. Why was she making such a big deal out of this, anyway? She was not in the closet; she simply chose not to advertise her sexuality. Why risk being judged entirely in relation to one aspect of who she was as a person? That's what appalled her most about any form of prejudice.

Blair abandoned her unpacking and moved to the

windows, drawn by the tranquillity of green grass and shady trees. She could see why Cassie pined for her home.

Cassie threw her bag on her bed and spun around her room, grazing the familiar furniture with one hand. "I am so glad to be home," she informed the old dolls arranged along the top shelf of her bookcase.

When she had turned sixteen, she'd consigned the trappings of her childhood to a box in the attic. But it had seemed a betrayal of sorts to retire her dolls to darkness and dust, after years of cheerful service. So she had dressed each in her best outfit and placed them side by side on the wall opposite the window. One day she too would outlive her usefulness, Cassie told herself, and she would be glad of a room with a view.

Humming to herself, she fossicked in her suitcase until she located the red billfold in which she kept her savings. Removing five hundred dollars, she stuffed the notes in her hip pocket, dragged a brush through her hair and followed the smell of warm scones to the kitchen.

"I've got something for you," she told her mother. "Close your eyes and put out your hand."

"I hope you haven't wasted your money on perfume or chocolates, Cassie Jensen." There was a hint of genuine consternation beneath the lightness.

As far back as Cassie could remember, her mother had deplored what she considered waste or extravagance. Glancing about the kitchen, Cassie had a flash of herself as a small child, standing on a chair, watching her mother boil down soap. Faith Jensen could never bring herself to discard the remains of a bar, even now accumulating these in a small jar in each bathroom.

Conscious of a guilty pleasure at the brand new soaps waiting their turn inside her bathroom cabinet back in Melbourne, Cassie placed the bundle of cash in her mother's outstretched hand.

"What's this?" Her mother blinked down at the gift. "Robbed a bank?"

Cassie grinned. "It'll be more next time. I'll ransom a clerk as well."

"You don't have to give me the money you earn, Cassie." Her mother was serious all of a sudden.

"I know that. But I want to. Just for while . . . till things get better." Cassie reached out and closed her mother's hand over the bills. "We are a family of two," she repeated one of her mother's frequent homilies. "We are not less because we are few."

"We are two who love," Faith Jensen huskily completed. Tucking the money into her apron, she said, "Fetch your friend, Cassie. It's time we ate those scones."

The late afternoon was suffocatingly hot. Cassie had succumbed soon after lunch, vanishing to her room to take a nap. Left sharing the veranda with Faith, Blair sipped her iced tea and allowed her mind to drift. It would be two in the morning in New York. Lisa would be sound asleep, smelling of Estee

Lauder face cream and snoring lightly. Beside her, instead of Blair, would be Sue.

With any luck, they'd have had lousy sex, but somehow Blair doubted it. They had probably spent hours swimming in each other. Perhaps they were perfectly matched, in a way she and Lisa never were, but wanted to be, as if wanting were enough. It was more than some people had.

Blair frowned slightly. She had always assessed her relationship that way, by comparing it with someone else's miserable failure. Her mother had done the same thing, dismissing criticism of her husband's behavior with the rejoinder, "at least he doesn't beat me".

Blair had always promised herself she would not have a relationship as barren as her parents'. They were still together, their complete indifference to each other a habit they described as "getting on fine". It was true that they seldom fought anymore. They had solved disappointment by lowering their expectations. The adventure and possibility of the unknown no longer seemed more alluring than the comfort and predictability of the life they had crafted together. They had settled for a tidy house, a shiny car and a Florida vacation every second summer.

Blair waved her rice paper fan, batting away several lethargic flies that were circling her. She and Lisa had been happy, she supposed — if the absence of unhappiness were any kind of yardstick. What if they had stayed together — another twenty years of passive contentment? It didn't sound so bad. There were lonely people all over the world who would be thrilled at the idea.

Blair glanced toward Faith Jensen. Was she hoping to meet someone? She was only in her early fifties, and clearly an attractive, interesting woman.

As if sensing her appraisal, Faith looked up from the dense paperback she was reading. "Delia tells me you broke up with your partner a few months ago," she said, very forthright.

"I was just thinking about that," Blair admitted, somewhat taken aback.

"I thought you might have been. Strange, isn't it, at first — getting used to being alone?"

"It took a while to sink in," Blair said. "At first I thought she'd come back."

"I understand," Faith said. "I lost my husband nearly five years ago. Sometimes I still expect to see him walk in that gate come sunset. He used to sit there, where you are now."

Blair stiffened, uncertain how to respond to this knowledge. Her first impulse was to vacate the wicker chair. Instead, she said, "You must miss him," and immediately berated herself for such a feeble comment.

"Very much," Faith replied. "He was my one and only."

It was so simply stated, and with such absolute conviction, Blair found herself speechless.

"Most people find that hard to conceive of," Faith continued. "But it's something I know is true for myself."

"Does that mean you'll never give anyone else the chance?" Blair asked.

"I'd like to meet someone I could enjoy spending time with," Faith responded. "But it's not quite the same thing. You see, James was my passion. We belonged together. If I met someone else, I would hope for a good friendship."

"Love?"

"Perhaps. If I'm fortunate."

"But not this . . . passion?"

Faith seemed surprised at the very suggestion. "How could I? I still feel it for James."

Blair contemplated the hazy sky. High above, seemingly painted against the washed-out blue, a wedge-tailed eagle rode a thermal. "Do you think it's a once-in-a-lifetime thing?" she asked.

"I really don't know," Faith replied eventually. "Once was enough for me."

* * * * *

Cassie was half awake, the memory of a dream clinging, cobweb-like. Something to do with Blair. Cassie rolled onto her back, allowing her mind to float toward unconsciousness. As she slid into half-sleep, she found herself mentally watching two women, one in the other's lap. Only it wasn't Jude and Nan. It was herself on Blair's knee, her arms around Blair's neck, her mouth against Blair's.

Cassie sat bolt upright, taking comfort in the familiar pattern of her pale green wallpaper, the sound of cockys calling. Softly, from the front veranda, she could hear voices. Blair and her mother. She slid beneath her quilt again, cheeks warming as she reviewed the subject of her dream.

The heat from her face traveled down her neck and seemed to lodge between her thighs. Feeling a slippery sensation as she parted her legs, Cassie wondered for a moment if she had got her period. It was impossible. She was never this early.

Blood rushed in her ears. Physical arousal. Recently, she had noticed such cravings more often. In a job like hers it was inevitable you'd end up with sex on the brain, she supposed. Yet it was not like that at all. She could think of nothing less exciting than some of the activities she heard Nan and Jude describing. If anything, she found her work a complete turn-off.

Yet, when she was at home, she was often aware of a physical restlessness, her body dictating yearnings she could barely understand, much less satisfy. Curious, she had investigated the vibrators Antoinette stocked to sell to the escorts. Perhaps she should buy one, she thought. Stroking herself with her fingers only seemed to make everything worse.

Laughter filtered its way through her window. She could just discern Blair's voice. Again she thought about that dream. She could almost feel Blair against her. There was something very delicious about the fantasy. Cassie closed her eyes, extending it a little: Blair kissing her neck, stroking her breasts.

Abruptly, her eyes flew open. Gazing at her from the opposite wall, her dolls seemed as dumbstruck as she was.

"Blair," Cassie whispered. Her stomach lurched in response.

CHAPTER NINE

She had a tiny dark mole on her left shoulder, visible when her singlet slid back. Along her forearms a down of fine pale hairs picked up the sun. Her hands were darker than the throat they stroked occasionally, an absent-minded gesture Cassie had often seen, but never watched.

Her earlobes were perfect, neatly encircled with thick little gold crescents. When she smiled the lines beneath her eyes deepened. She wore no make-up but periodically applied a lip balm from a tiny pot she carried in her pocket. Her mouth was a no-nonsense kind of straight. Cassie wondered how it would feel on hers.

"Have I got something on my teeth?" Blair asked.

Cassie hastily lowered her gaze. "I'm sorry. I was . . . just thinking."

"Thinking what?" Blair asked lightly.

If only you knew. Cassie poured milk onto her cereal. Her hand felt unsteady, as though the strength had ebbed from her wrist and at any moment she would drop the pitcher. Returning it to the table with a slight thud, she said, "I was thinking I could show you 'round the farm today."

"That's a good idea, darling." Her mom appeared with a plate of scrambled eggs. "You could take the pickup and check for stragglers in the eastern paddocks."

Blair seemed enthusiastic. "Will you come with us, Faith?"

"No. I've got the vet coming over this morning." She piled egg onto a slice of toast and handed it to Cassie, who felt her stomach roll at the sight. "Everything okay, dear?" her mother asked.

Catching an inquisitive look from Blair, Cassie said, "I'm fine." Forcing a smile, she took the plate and made a show of sprinkling salt and pepper over the curdled yellow mess.

"Perhaps you should stay in," Blair commented with concern. "You could probably do with a rest. I could take a walk . . ."

"No," Cassie said abruptly. "I'm fine. Honestly."

Her companions exchanged a glance.

"I'm concerned about this night shift business, Cassie," her mother said. "Could you change to something in the daytime when you get back?"

What had Blair been saying? Cassie shook her head. "They've got daytime staff, Mom. I don't mind nights, anyway. I'm used to it now."

"I worry about you being out late in the city."

Cassie groaned. "Oh, Mom —"

Her mother lifted a hand. "I don't like to think of you taking taxis all over town when it's dark. Anything could happen."

"I think your mother has a point," Blair said, blatantly ignoring Cassie's accusing stare. "You're not used to being in the city yet. Just the other day, you hadn't put the bolts on when you went to bed —"

"I'm not a child." Cassie placed her knife and fork down with a clatter. "I'll be twenty soon. I —"

All three women turned at the sound of a vehicle.

"That must be the vet." Faith Jensen stood.

As soon as she'd left the room, Cassie turned to Blair. "What have you been saying to her?"

Blair raised an eyebrow. "I have been the model of discretion, Cassie. But I could hardly refuse to answer your mom's questions."

"You could tell her to talk to me," Cassie said indignantly.

Blair looked exasperated. "I did."

"I thought you were on my side." Cassie folded her arms, staring flintily out the window. She heard her mother return, and out of the corner of her eye saw a second person.

"— so, please join us for a cup of tea," Faith said, adding as Cassie turned, "This is my daughter Cassie, and a friend of the family, Blair Carroll, from New York. This is our locum vet, Marla Farrant."

A blond woman advanced into the room, her hand outstretched to Blair. "I'm delighted to meet you," she said in an English accent. "I was in New York City myself, back in June."

"Really?" Blair was on her feet, apparently as interested in Marla as Marla seemed to be in Blair. "Business or pleasure."

"Strictly pleasure." Marla withdrew her hand, but her bright blue eyes lingered on Blair a moment longer, before flicking toward Cassie, whom she greeted with a dismissive smile.

"Marla is looking after Bill's practice while he's visiting his parents in Ireland," Faith Jensen explained. "How are the locals coping?"

Marla sat down where she was shown and heaved a theatrical sigh. "Well, they're certainly not used to dealing with a woman."

"Much less one who looks like you." Faith laughed.

"You know —" Marla confided. "I can handle the men. They get embarrassed easily and they don't say much. But frankly, the worst problem I've had is with your neighbors."

"The Murphys?"

Marla smoothed her hair. "I feel quite sorry for those girls, Faith. I heard they've run wild since they were young. But really —"

Cassie could picture the Murphy sisters' response to the arrival of an attractive female vet in the neighborhood. "You'd better watch out," she warned their visitor. "Don't let them see you at the snake farm."

Marla gazed blankly from Cassie to her mother.

"Cassie's right," Faith agreed reluctantly. "The sisters have set their sights on the owner. They're a little possessive."

"Obsessive," Cassie corrected, adding with a certain relish, "They'd shoot you soon as look at you."

Blair seemed disbelieving. "Are you saying these women are both after the same guy, and they don't want any competition?"

"Well, they don't have any from me." Marla's laughter was tinged with uncertainty. "I'm not the least bit interested in their snake farmer."

"And he's not the least bit interested in them." Faith observed. "But, the girls are —"

"They're not playing with a full deck," Cassie explained.

"Cassie . . ."

"It's the truth, Mom," Cassie protested. "I should know. I had to go to school with them."

Marla seemed nonplussed. "You can't seriously think they would harm me."

"Cassie is exaggerating a little," Faith Jensen assured the vet. "You've got nothing to worry about, so long as you stay well clear of Tommy Bryce."

"I'm calling on him after I've finished with your sheep," Marla said. "He's got some anti-venom for us."

"Watch your back," Cassie muttered.

"You took a dislike to Marla, didn't you?" Blair asked as she and Cassie bounced along the eastern boundary of the property.

Staring fixedly ahead, Cassie said, "What makes you think that?"

Blair hesitated. She was still trying to fathom

Cassie's mood. Over breakfast, she had seemed alternately self-conscious and prickly, and as for her behavior toward the delicious vet — her animosity had been palpable. "You frightened her deliberately."

"She'll get over it, Cassie said in a flat tone.

Blair slowed down, shooting a sidelong glance at her passenger. "What happened to country hospitality?"

Cassie was silent, her profile set stubbornly.

"Something's bugging you." Blair made an effort to stifle her mounting irritation. "Wanna tell me about it?"

"It's nothing," Cassie replied.

"Are you upset that your mom couldn't come?" Simple resentment could explain Cassie's behavior, Blair decided. She was quite probably reluctant to share her mother during the brief time she was visiting, and she had taken out her frustration on the vet.

"I was telling the truth about the Murphy sisters," Cassie said huffily.

"I'm sure you were." Blair was suddenly flooded with feeling for the young woman. She could imagine, seeing the ravaged property, how stressful the past few years must have been for Cassie and her mother. They were both reacting in their own different ways to the changes hardship had imposed on them.

Blair pulled over into the feeble shade cast by a group of ragged looking mallee trees. Touching Cassie's shoulder, she said, "I know this is a hard time for you."

Cassie turned slowly, her eyes bright with tears. "I don't know what to do," she said in a soft, choked voice. "Everything is such a mess."

"I know." Blair slid across the seat and placed a consoling arm around her shoulders. Stroking her hair, she said, "You're doing everything you can, Cassie. You couldn't do any more."

Cassie sagged against her, "It's not just the farm," she said. "It's everything else. It's all so confusing."

Blair took Cassie's hot face gently between her hands and looked into her eyes. "Life is like that," she said. "It never stops being confusing. Trust me." She planted a kiss lightly on Cassie's forehead and released her, slightly startled when she felt one of her hands caught.

"Blair." Cassie searched her face earnestly. "Do you like me?"

"Of course I do."

"I mean really like me."

Something in her expression jolted Blair. In the same moment she became aware of her hand in Cassie's, Cassie's thumb tracing the outline of her knuckles.

Blair gazed down at their linked hands. Cassie's breasts rose and fell quickly beneath her cotton shirt. The air-conditioner droned. "I'm not sure what you're asking me," she said, knowing she would have been sure in any other circumstances. But was Cassie aware of what she doing?

"Cassie," Blair said. "There's something I need to tell you."

Cassie's gaze was unwavering.

"I'm a lesbian." Blair held her breath for a split-second. To her complete surprise Cassie's face immediately lost its frozen concentration.

"A lesbian," she repeated. "Really?"

"Yes, really."

Cassie's patent relief was not quite the reaction Blair had anticipated. Neither was her next response. Cassie Jensen burst out laughing.

"What's so funny?" Blair demanded.

"Nothing. Nothing at all." Cassie was obviously having trouble containing herself. "I . . . um. Thanks for telling me."

Biting back a sarcastic response, Blair turned on the motor, threw the pickup into gear and backed into the blazing sunlight. In the half hour drive that followed, Cassie burst into laughter several times. On each occasion, she insisted nothing was wrong. She said she was amazed that Blair could have been worried about telling her. She was relieved that she now knew, and horrified that she might have offended Blair with speculation about husbands and men friends.

In Blair's experience coming out had never been like this. Her mother had responded with a frozen silence that had taken four years to thaw. Her father still made like he'd never heard anything about it. Her two brothers, much younger than Blair, didn't express strong feelings about anything except football, so she had no idea what they thought. Friends and colleagues seemed comfortable enough, but Blair refrained from telling anyone she suspected might find her sexuality a problem.

Cassie was the first person who had ever greeted the news as if it were welcome, albeit something of a non-event.

"I work with two lesbians," she informed Blair cheerfully. "I only found out last week. Wait till I tell them about you."

"There's no need to advertise it," Blair said.

"Are you . . . er, in the closet?"

"No," Blair said, niggled.

"I'm not criticizing," Cassie went on. "I know some people have a real problem with it. Bizarre isn't it? I mean, it couldn't possibly be as weird as some of the stuff so called normal people get up to."

And what would you know about that? Blair glanced across at Cassie's placid countenance. "It's not all about sex, you know."

Cassie fell silent.

"I mean, there's more to sexual orientation than who you want to sleep with." Blair was conscious she sounded patronizing.

"Like what?" Cassie asked. "I mean, isn't that how you can tell. You want to have sex with a woman, right? So you're a lesbian. And the Murphy sisters want to do it with the snake farmer. And they're plain crazy, but that's beside the point. They're heterosexuals, right?"

"Well, it's kind of simplistic." Blair laughed in spite of herself. "But I guess you could put it that way."

"So, if I wanted to kiss a woman," Cassie concluded on an odd note, "that would make me a lesbian."

"Not so fast," Blair said, sensing slippery ground. "It's more complex than that. For a start, you're only nineteen. You might think about kissing a woman, or a man . . . exploring your feelings."

"What if the woman I wanted to kiss was a lesbian? What if —"

A sharp explosion sounded somewhere nearby, followed immediately by another.

101

"That sounded like gunshots." Blair braked hard and pulled off her sunglasses.

Cassie was staring intently out her window. "Damn right it was. And it looks like it's not rabbits they're aiming for, either." She pointed at a speck in the distance. "That's a vehicle."

Blair fumbled in the back seat, locating her binoculars. "Strange," she said as she trained the lenses on a stationary orange pickup she recognized. "It's Marla."

Marla Farrant was lying hunched on the floor of the cab. At first glance, Cassie thought she was dead. Banging on the locked driver's door, she yelled, "Marla. Open up."

The blond head lifted and pushing her hair off her pale face, Marla Farrant scrambled onto the seat and opened the door. "Thank God it's you." She stared frantically around. "Someone took a shot at me."

Blair's mouth was thin, her gray eyes chill with anger. "Did you see who it was?"

Marla raised a shaking hand, gesturing vaguely east. "I was crossing the creek bed over there. It just came out of nowhere. I think one of them hit the back of the truck."

Cassie had already found the hole, close to the right rear wheel. "Looks like they tried for a tire," she remarked.

"You know, I thought you were joking about those girls," Marla said weakly.

"A breakdown out here is no joke," Blair

commented. "You'd last about a day. Two if you had plenty of water."

Marla looked like she was about to faint.

"I'll get you a drink," Cassie said, scanning the plains for any sign of another truck. "You'd better sit down."

Leaving Blair to prop Marla in what little shade her pickup offered, Cassie siphoned some water from the large vacuum tank stored beneath the front seat of the Land Cruiser. Despite the Murphys' reputation, even Cassie was having a hard time imagining the sisters taking pot shots at the locum vet. She stole a glance at Marla, prickling slightly at the protective stance Blair had assumed.

Handing Marla a cup of water, she said, "Why don't you drive Marla back to the homestead, Blair. I'm going to pay a call on the neighbors."

"Do you think that's wise?" Blair wiped her sunglasses on her shirt, then put them on again.

"They're not going to shoot me," Cassie said. "They pump their water supply from one of our bores."

CHAPTER TEN

The Murphy sisters were adamant. They had nothing to do with the shooting. For a start, if they'd wanted to nail that scrawny blond sheila they'd have put one right between the eyes, they advised Cassie.

"Bet she got a fright, eh?" Shirl, the older of the two, sniggered as she buttered some bread. "That'll learn 'er."

"You like Melbourne?" Lindy, the younger, asked.

Cassie glanced around their malodorous kitchen. A hole had been knocked out in the far wall.

Conveniently, this led straight through to the piggery, enabling the effortless transportation of food scraps. When the Murphys had callers, they placed a makeshift gate across this passage to keep the inquisitive pigs back.

Lifting her voice over the grunts and squeals of protest, Cassie said, "Melbourne's great. I've got a job."

Shirl seemed unimpressed. Licking butter off her fingers, she asked, "Boyfriend?"

Cassie shook her head, trying not to flinch as Lindy sprinkled the heavily buttered bread with sugar. "I don't really have the time."

"You never had a boyfriend," Shirl reminded her.

"I don't want a boyfriend," Cassie retorted, irritated to find herself participating in this schoolyard game.

"Poppy got sixteen piglets," Lindy announced with satisfaction, honoring Cassie by serving the sugared bread on the best china.

"Sixteen." Cassie whistled. "All surviving?"

Shirl opened a cupboard beside the kitchen sink and extracted a squirming pink piglet. "Runt," she explained, tucking the animal inside her shapeless cardigan.

"So, you haven't been out Narrung way this afternoon?" Cassie asked, politely nibbling her bread.

The Murphys shot each other darting looks.

"We seen 'er," Lindy admitted.

"Down Tommy's." Shirl nodded in the direction of the snake farm.

"I want to see your shotguns," Cassie said. "If you're telling lies . . ."

Lindy shook her head vehemently. "No lies, Cassie." Her eyes brimming with tears, she thrust another slice of bread at Cassie's chest.

"It's her time," Shirl offered blandly. "We like Libra. It's thin."

The Murphy sisters had used rags for their menstruation until Cassie's mother revolutionized their monthly cycles by introducing them to the sanitary towel. In the years that followed, they had tried every known brand, and conveyed their findings whenever Cassie saw them.

"Show me the guns." Cassie directed the sisters back to the topic.

Shirl handed the piglet to Lindy, who dipped her fingers into the milk pitcher and allowed the animal to suck them. When she returned, Shirl carried half a dozen shotguns and an automatic pistol. They were all cold and showed no signs of recent discharge.

Frowning, Cassie asked, "Is this all?"

"We never shot 'er," Lindy said.

"Reckon it was 'im," Shirl continued. "In the Jackaroo."

"Who?" Cassie asked. "What Jackaroo?"

"Dunno. Not from 'round 'ere." Shirl took the piglet from Lindy, kissing its snout.

Frustrated, Cassie said, "So you saw a man driving a Jackaroo?"

"It was 'im shot her, Cassie." Lindy wiped her hands on her chest. "We seen 'im."

Cassie stared at the fat stained ceiling and counted to three. "Now you tell me," she muttered.

* * * * *

By the time Cassie had finished describing her interaction with the Murphy sisters, Marla's face had turned the color of whey.

"Do you know this guy?" Blair asked her.

"I can't believe he's found me." Marla was visibly trembling. "Out here, of all the Godforsaken places."

Marla had left England to get away from a former boyfriend who was obsessed with her. Assuming a new name, she had worked in Sydney for two years. One day he had walked into her veterinary clinic and kidnapped her at knifepoint.

"I played along with him," Marla said. "I didn't think it would work, but after a couple of hours he relaxed a bit. Then I said I was hungry and hadn't eaten all day and he took me to a restaurant. I wrote a note under the table and passed it to the waitress. They called the police."

It sounded like television, Cassie thought, only it was real. Their glamorous vet was being stalked. "What happened? Did he go to jail?"

"He got a suspended sentence," Marla replied bitterly. "He's a doctor. He bought a top lawyer and a couple of expert witnesses who said he'd had a breakdown and was acting out of character." She managed a half-laugh. "They made me out to be some kind of siren. I think they got their ideas from *Basic Instinct*."

"And now he's found you again." Blair paced the veranda, apparently deep in concentration.

"He's watching me," Marla said, slender hands clenching compulsively. "Oh God, I'm so sick of this."

Guiltily Cassie remembered her own attempt to frighten Marla earlier that day. How could she have been so thoughtless?

"Did the court issue a restraining order?" Blair asked.

"He said he was going back to England." Marla dragged a weary hand through her hair. "Look, I'm sorry about this. There's no reason why you should get involved. I can sort it out."

"What are you going to do?" Faith asked. "You can't keep moving to a new town and changing your name. What about your career? Your family?"

"That's how he caught up with me in the first place," Marla said. "I didn't communicate with anyone when I moved to Sydney. Not even my mother. No one knew where I was. After a year, I phoned home at Christmas time. Mother said he'd moved to Yorkshire, so I started writing to her. As it turned out, he'd hired a private detective to find me. The police said that's quite common."

"Do you think he was trying to kill you, this afternoon?" Blair asked quietly.

"I think he was trying to make me stop the truck. After that, I don't know . . ." She shuddered.

"You can't go back to your house alone," Blair said. "If it's okay with you, Faith . . ."

"You must stay here, Marla," Faith said briskly. With a quick warning look at Cassie, she added, "You can have Cassie's room. We can put a fold-out bed in the sun porch."

"There's a spare bed in my room," Blair said without inflection. "Cassie can share with me."

Well, thanks for organizing my life like I'm not here, Cassie thought. There was worse to come.

"We'll be traveling back to Melbourne on Tuesday." Blair's tone softened as she spoke to Marla. "I think you should come with us."

"But what about the practice? Bill won't be back for three weeks."

Faith patted Marla's hand. "No worries. Old man Kimball, down Wombat Creek, used to be the vet round here. We can haul him out of retirement until we get someone else."

Marla looked bemused, her blue eyes shifting from Cassie to her mother, then to Blair, who seemed oddly unfazed by the entire bizarre situation.

"Those Murphy sisters —" Blair directed her attention to Cassie. "What kind of truck do they drive?"

"A clapped-out Range Rover." Cassie wondered what she had in mind.

"And they'd like Marla out of the picture, right?" At Cassie's cautious nod, Blair smiled. "Marla," she said. "We need the keys to your apartment and a list of everything you want packed."

"You're serious," Marla said.

Blair gave a brief shrug. "Under the circumstances, yes."

CHAPTER ELEVEN

"I can't believe we're doing this," Cassie said as she and Blair bundled clothing into Marla Farrant's suitcases. "Can't we just call the police or something?"

"Do you read the newspapers, Cassie?" Blair said. "There are women all over the world who would still be alive if the law offered adequate protection."

"But he's ruined her life." Cassie was appalled. "He should be made to pay."

"I agree," Blair said. "But Marla has to be kept safe until that happens."

"What are we going to do with her?" Cassie demanded. "We've only got two bedrooms in the flat."

Blair looked impatient. "We'll work something out. She can stay in a hotel. Whatever. I don't know."

"Why us? Why do we have to play hero?"

"I have no idea," Blair said. "All I know is that we got involved. What would you have preferred? To leave her out there terrified in her jeep?"

"Don't be ridiculous." Cassie slammed her bag closed and examined the neatly written list Marla had provided. "This is Australia. We don't walk away from people."

"Then what's the problem, exactly?"

Cassie had asked herself the very same question. Normally she wouldn't hesitate to give someone a helping hand. But she was irked at the very idea that Marla would be coming back to Melbourne with them.

Blair examined her with quizzical gray eyes. "You're jealous, aren't you, Cassie. You're used to being your mom's center of attention, and now, thanks to Marla, and me too, I suppose, your weekend has been ruined. Grow up, for God's sake."

"It's not that at all." Cassie felt a lump jamming her throat. "You don't understand." Grabbing another suitcase, she began collecting the cosmetics on Marla's dressing table. She could feel Blair's gaze.

"What don't I understand?" Blair's tone was suddenly more gentle.

Cassie wished she could articulate exactly what she felt, but her thoughts would follow no logical sequence. "It's got nothing to do with Marla." She was unable to meet Blair's steady regard. "I don't know what's wrong with me."

"How about easing up on yourself," Blair suggested, her expression softening.

Cassie looked away, but not before guilty heat had swamped her cheeks. She wanted to kiss Blair. She hoped it was not written all over her face.

In shifts, they lugged Marla's gear to the Murphys' Range Rover.

"I still don't think we needed to borrow this," Cassie said. "I think you're being paranoid."

"I'm being realistic." Blair said impatiently. "This guy has been hunting Marla for several years. If he's watching this place, he could easily take down the number of your mom's truck and trace it back to Narrung. Is that what you want?"

"What if he traces the Range Rover back to the Murphys."

Blair slammed the doors shut on their cargo. "I imagine the Murphy sisters would know how to deal with him," she said mildly.

"I really don't understand it," Cassie got into the truck. "The men who do this. They must be sick."

Blair reached across her, locking the passenger door. "Their behavior is completely in line with a culture in which women are treated as possessions. Pornography, prostitution, domestic violence, sexual harassment. They all stem from the same ideology. It's known as the patriarchy."

"You're a feminist too, then?" Cassie asked.

"I'm pro-woman," Blair said. "You can give it any label you like, sweetheart."

* * * * *

Marla had already gone to bed when they got

back to Narrung. Faith helped them unload the Range Rover.

"We'll take it back in the morning," Cassie said. "I told the sisters we'd be too late tonight."

Blair parked in the garage, then followed the others indoors.

"Are you quite sure you don't want me to organize that fold-out bed?" Faith asked.

Blair glanced at Cassie, who gave a self-conscious shrug and said, "I don't mind the stretcher, if you'd rather be alone."

"Do you snore?" Blair teased.

Cassie did not join her mother's laughter. "I'm taking a shower," she said and stalked off.

Faith smiled after her. "She doesn't snore," she informed Blair. "But she does talk in her sleep."

Blair grinned. "Thanks for the warning."

It felt odd, Blair reflected as she showered — Faith's obvious unconcern that her teenage daughter would be sharing a room with a lesbian. Of course, there was no reason why she should feel concerned. That was exactly what Blair found most astonishing. Faith simply treated her like any other human being. She trusted Blair, the person. Sexuality was irrelevant.

No wonder Cassie had seemed so casual about Blair's announcement of her lesbianism. Clearly Faith Jensen's refreshing lack of homophobia had communicated itself to her daughter. Faith must have come to terms with her sister Delia's unusual lifestyle some time ago. Lesbianism was probably small fry by comparison with a husband who cross-dressed and had his boyfriend sharing the house.

Cassie was hovering between the twin beds when

Blair emerged from the bathroom. "I wasn't sure which one . . ." she said, fingers straying to the top button of her nightshirt.

"I'm by the window," Blair replied.

Dutifully Cassie climbed beneath the covers of her assigned bed. Her cheeks were flushed from showering. Damp corkscrew tendrils clung to her face and neck. Rubbing her hand across her mouth, she said, "Did you have a nice shower, Blair?"

Blair groaned inwardly at the forced small talk. It was okay driving with a lesbian, but sleeping in the same room was quite another matter, it seemed. Making a minimalist reply, Blair set her alarm clock, checked that the window was fastened and pulled back her covers. She could feel Cassie staring.

"Is something wrong?" she inquired, sliding into bed and rolling onto her side to face her roommate.

Cassie shook her head, wet curls bouncing like loosely coiled springs. She was still sitting up, her expression one of wide-eyed apprehension.

Blair guessed at the cause. "Are you scared this guy's gonna show up here?"

Cassie gazed at her with the polite incomprehension of a foreigner listening to directions. "Er . . . no," she said and promptly lay down, as if she had just worked out that this was what she was supposed to do.

"So, you're okay?"

"I'm fine."

They might have been strangers finding themselves in adjoining seats on a plane.

Blair sighed. "Cassie, if I were planning to molest you in your sleep I've had plenty of opportunity before today."

Cassie's pink cheeks turned red.

"Get some sleep," Blair said wearily. Exasperation drove her to add, "This is exactly the reason I didn't tell you weeks ago."

The guilty red tide proceeded down Cassie's neck.

Lay off the kid, Blair told herself. How many nineteen-year-olds could instantly come to grips with their feelings? After a day like the one they'd just been through, it was little wonder Cassie seemed shell-shocked.

Cassie went through the stalling motions of rearranging her pillows and quilt.

Blair sensed her uncertainty. "I'm sorry," she said. "I guess I'm finding this stressful too."

Her softer tone was rewarded with a timid half-smile. "I'm sorry too," Cassie said.

"Shall I put out the light?" Blair asked.

"Yes, please."

Blair flicked the switch and removed the soft cotton T-shirt that doubled as pajamas. She could hear Cassie fidgeting with her bedding. "Goodnight, Cassie," she said.

"Blair?"

"Yes."

There was a pause. "It doesn't matter. It's just another dumb question."

"Spit it out, then," Blair invited. She was certain she heard Cassie take a breath.

"Have you ever thought about having sex with me, Blair?" The question reverberated like footsteps in an alley.

"I'm not sure I can answer that." Blair was careful to make her tone light. "I could say no, and you might feel undesirable, which would be ridiculous, because you are a very attractive woman. Or I could say yes, and you might run screaming from the bed. Then your mother would throw me out and I would get back to Melbourne only to find my possessions on the street and new locks on the door."

She was relieved to hear Cassie laughing. "I had no idea it was so complicated."

"Well, what would you say?" Blair demanded. "Think about that."

There was a scuffling sound and the lamp went on. Cassie was standing over Blair. She knelt, resting her arms and head on the edge of the bed. "I have," she said. "I had a dream that you kissed me. I was sitting on your knee."

With her ear against the pillow, Blair could hear her heart thudding. She inhaled Cassie's mild rosy scent. She had no idea what to say. "Are you hitting on me, Cassie?" She managed to sound more casual than she felt.

Cassie raised her head, propping her chin between her hands. "Do you want me to?"

The challenge was unmistakable. Blair could remember playing chicken with her own emotions at that age, determined, at the risk of burns, to find out how much heat she could stand. Cassie would withdraw in a flash as soon as she reached the outer limit of her comfort zone.

Collecting a dark curl around her index finger, Blair said, "I've thought about kissing you."

"I thought about you kissing my mouth and my neck and my breasts," Cassie said, her face sliding into Blair's hand.

Blair tried to slow her shallow breathing. "I've thought about you naked."

Cassie rocked back on her heels, calmly undoing her nightshirt.

Blair arrested her hands. The game had gone far enough. "Cassie —"

"I want you to kiss me."

Blair studied Cassie's full mouth. "I'd want more than kisses." Abruptly she released Cassie's hands, rolling onto her back and staring at the ceiling. This was happening way too fast.

Cassie stood. As Blair looked on she pulled her nightshirt over her head. Naked, she said, "Can I get into bed with you?"

With only the barest hesitation, Blair lifted the bedding so that Cassie could slide beneath it.

"I've never done this," Cassie said. "Not with anyone. Not even kissing."

Blair rolled to face her. "Well, I have to tell you —" She brushed Cassie's mouth lightly with her own. "Your seduction technique is excellent, for a novice." Drawing Cassie into her arms, she placed chaste kisses on her forehead and cheeks.

She felt like throwing Cassie onto her back and crawling all over her, pushing into her soft places, exacting cries of shock and pleasure. Instead she embarked on an exploration so restrained it was almost excruciating. She wound her fingers into Cassie's hair, overcoming its silky resistance. Cradling her head she kissed the corners of her mouth, teasing it apart.

Cassie was shivering, her fingers pressing into Blair's shoulders. "Blair," she whispered against her mouth. "What do you want me to do?"

Between slow kisses, Blair replied, "Anything you want, Cassie." She lowered her mouth to Cassie's throat, biting softly, then drew back a little to study her breasts. They were very full, her nipples dark and puckered as raisins. Blair touched them delicately, until the surrounding skin began to pull and wrinkle too. "You're beautiful," she said, rolling Cassie gently onto her back and kneeling beside her.

Cassie stared up, trust and apprehension laced with yearning. Her breathing was shallow. Wetting her mouth, she reached for Blair, pulling her determinedly down.

Blair did not resist. Sliding a thigh between Cassie's legs, she lay over her, allowing their bodies to connect fully. Her skin felt very hot. So did her mouth. At first Cassie kissed a little uncertainly, her hands stroking Blair's back, shaking slightly. Then Blair felt her legs parting, the increasing pressure of her hands. Her body moved against Blair's, inviting, supplicant. Blair felt the rush and pound of desire, the ache that overtook caution or resolve.

Deepening her kisses, she pressed her hand into the warm hollow between Cassie's legs, kneading with the ball of her thumb, fingers separating the slippery matte of dark hair. Cassie clasped her shoulders, releasing small torn gasps as Blair eased her fingers back and forth.

She yearned to taste Cassie, to bury her face in the juicy sweetness that saturated her fingers. But Cassie's deepening pleasure was so profound, she was reluctant to do anything that might unnerve her. Reveling instead in the heat and salt-sweet scent of her, she worked the folds of skin that encased Cassie's clitoris, until its tender head was exposed.

Cassie tilted her head back, surrendering herself to sensation. She was made for this, Blair found herself thinking as she concentrated on that tiny pleasure center. Her body was so welcoming, so solid and warm and womanly. Resting her head between Cassie's breasts and listening to the thud of her heart, Blair felt a flutter of uncertainty. Pain caught at her chest. Cassie was so completely different from Lisa. Everywhere. Every way. Making love to her, Blair felt oddly vulnerable.

Her mind ran on. Maybe this was a mistake. Maybe Cassie would be disappointed. Nineteen-year-olds experimented. Maybe she would regret this. Blair wasn't sure if she could cope with that. She became conscious of Cassie stroking her hair, of her reassuring warmth. Lifting her head, Blair sought out Cassie's eyes. Their expression jolted her — desire; simple and unselfconscious.

Almost deliberately, Cassie arched her back and lifted her knees. Reading her body language as an invitation, Blair slid deliciously downward, maneuvering herself into position between her legs.

Conscious of Cassie tensing as warm air was blown between her thighs, Blair withdrew gently, instead gathering her close and kissing her throat, "You're beautiful," she whispered. "I want to taste you. Can I do that?"

As Cassie nodded, she slipped a hand between her legs, gathering fluids with her fingertips. She brought these to her mouth and sucked and licked, watching emotion play across Cassie's features. Shyness, embarrassed delight.

"Can I touch you, too?" Cassie asked.

"I'd like that."

Cassie hesitated. "Shall I get my vibrator?"

"What?"

Laughing softly, Cassie nibbled Blair's ear. "I was joking."

Blair couldn't help herself. She started laughing, too. Wrestling Cassie down onto the sheets, she pinned her shoulders. "Cassie Jensen. I can't believe you said that."

"You expected more of a simpering virgin?" Cassie's eyes were wicked.

Blair laced her fingers between Cassie's and kissed her slowly and at length. "I don't know what to expect," she admitted eventually. "This feels pretty new to me, too."

Cassie smiled. "I like it, Blair."

Her sweet frankness filled Blair with a giddy sense of possibility. It was as if suddenly she could let go, and instead of falling she would float. Placing her mouth over Cassie's, she eased between her legs, and kissing her blindly, lost herself in the secrets of her body.

Much later, Blair gazed at the woman blissfully asleep in her arms and felt choked with emotion. Whatever happens, she thought, this is perfect.

CHAPTER TWELVE

Cassie had no idea where to look. Every time someone spoke to her she jumped.

"Are you all right, darling?" Her mother examined her strangely.

"Yes." Her voice came out like a squeak. She dared not meet Blair's eyes. She felt as if someone was announcing everything they had done the night before on a loud hailer. *Cassie Jensen discovered the female orgasm after several attempts. She then licked the clitoris of her aunt's best friend.*

"Did you sleep well?" Her mother politely asked their unexpected houseguest.

Marla Farrant certainly looked as if she'd had her beauty sleep, Cassie noted. She was one of those women who would look sensational in any fashion. Today, in tiny candy-striped shorts and flimsy cream cotton shirt, she could have passed for a model.

"I slept very well," Marla said. "I really can't thank you enough for doing this." Turning her attention to Blair, she added, "I don't want to put you out. I'm sure I can make other arrangements to travel to Melbourne."

Make them, Cassie wanted to shout.

But Blair seemed determined to save the damsel in distress. Casting a brief sidelong glance at Cassie, she said, "It's no problem, Marla. You'll be safest coming with us."

To Cassie's horror, Marla took Blair's hand. "Thank you. You've no idea how much it means to me to have your support."

This time Blair sent a distinctly warning glance at Cassie.

Was she that obvious? Cassie wondered. Her mother was eyeing her with frowning concern as well.

Setting her jaw and biting down on her lip, Cassie got up abruptly. "I'd best get the Range Rover back to the Murphys," she explained.

Spooning yogurt onto her cereal, Blair said, "If you can wait ten minutes, I'll drive you."

Cassie was dismayed to find her throat closing. "I feel like some time alone," she said hoarsely. "Enjoy your breakfast."

As she left the room, she heard her mother say

wryly, "Looks like that girl got out on the wrong side of the bed this morning." When someone coughed violently, she added, "Can I get you a glass of water, Blair?"

The Murphy sisters examined the Range Rover as if suspecting important parts might have been removed during its absence. Finally satisfied that their battered treasure was all in one piece, they invited Cassie indoors.

"Breakfast." Lindy pointed at the food laid out on the kitchen table. Through the hole in the wall, came demanding grunts and squeals, as the pigs detected a human presence.

Nauseous, Cassie surveyed an array of mutton chops, slippery underfried eggs and limp toast. The Murphys seldom had a visitor. Clearly they had prepared this extravagant feast in her honor.

"He was round 'ere," Shirl commented. "Him in the Jackaroo."

"When?" Cassie asked.

"Last night." Lindy wiped dust off a plate from their best china service and set it down in front of Cassie. "Shirl shot 'im."

Cassie found she could not take a breath.

"Missed the mongrel." Shirl sniffed.

Lindy made a noise like a hyena sneezing.

"What's so funny?" Shirl growled. "Eat up an' shut up." She shoved the mutton chops toward her sister.

"So . . . er, did you talk to him at all?" Cassie

asked, prying a slice of toast from the rack and determinedly buttering it. She tried to look grateful for the quivering egg Shirl plopped onto her plate.

Licking mutton grease off her fingers, Lindy said, "Came to the door. Nice-looking."

"He scarpered," Shirl said.

"That's probably a good thing." Cassie swallowed some egg without chewing. "It's best we let the police handle this."

Shirl looked dubious. "When's that vet shiela leaving?"

"Tomorrow," Cassie said. "Blair and I are driving her to Melbourne. She's going to stay with us for a few days."

"Is she coming back?" Lindy asked.

"I don't think so," Cassie said. "Now, if that guy in the Jackeroo comes around again, you mustn't say anything about Marla. He wants to hurt her."

The sisters nodded gravely.

Shirl paused in her chewing. "You want us to sort 'im out, Cass?"

"No. It's best you call my mom if you see him again. She'll take care of everything." She wiped her mouth carefully, and stood. "I must be going. Thanks for the breakfast. It was delicious."

The sisters followed her outdoors where they stood on their veranda, arms folded, mouths pink and shiny from the greasy food. Cassie felt a little guilty climbing into the pick-up, waving cheerfully. In twenty years time the Murphys would still be standing right there waving goodbye to someone. Their snake farmer, according to Cassie's mom, was on the brink of selling up and moving to Queensland.

The sisters would never leave Bendigo. Each

Christmas they would take a wagon of pigs to the market and both women would sob all the way home, as if they had just sold their children for slaughter.

Both girls had suffered mild brain damage at birth and their frail mother had died when Shirl was only five. Their father had entertained a succession of short-lived girlfriends, some of whom had cared for the sisters, others treated them worse than farm animals. In the end, Mr. Murphy had simply vanished one day.

Various rumors circulated in Bendigo — that he'd gone to Queensland and been taken by a shark, or that he'd fallen from his horse in a drunken stupor somewhere out on the property and died of exposure, or that maybe he'd run off to Sydney with his latest fancy woman. Who would have believed the truth? That he'd been shot in the head by fifteen-year-old Shirl, after years of sexually abusing both girls.

Shirl had butchered him, boiled him down and fed him to the pigs. His bones were buried six feet below the pig sty. Lindy knew nothing about it. Shirl had recently told Cassie's mom what she'd done and Faith Jensen had decided to do nothing. What was the point having Shirl locked up in a mental hospital over a 'crime' of self-defense? Faith had said to Cassie. Lindy would never manage alone.

Impulsively, Cassie climbed down from the pick-up. "I was thinking," she said to Shirl. "There's a breed of pig folks keep for pets, just like dogs."

"Pigs are smart," Lindy said.

"That's right. Anyway, these pigs are called Chinese pot bellied pigs. If you bred them you wouldn't have to sell them for eating."

The sisters squinted at her.

"You could change over gradually," Cassie explained. "Use the money from this year's sales to buy some breeding stock. Mom would help you."

"Chinese pigs." Shirl mused. "They fetch good money?"

"More than you get at the market," Cassie said.

Lindy nudged Shirl, who gave a dour nod and something approaching a smile.

Interpreting this as an enthusiastic yes, Cassie said, "I'll tell Mom to come on over and discuss it, then." On an impulse, she hugged each of them in turn, saying, "See you in a few weeks. Take care now."

The house was empty when Cassie arrived. Taking a pair of binoculars, she surveyed the surroundings. Her mother was ten minutes away, doing the feeding out in the southern paddocks. Usually these enclosures were reserved for the cashmere herd the farm had invested in several years ago, but the goats didn't seem to mind sharing their domain with a few hundred scrawny sheep.

Cassie drove out to the fenceline and tooted at her mother, who walked over to meet her.

"Where's Blair?" Cassie asked, jumping down from the pick-up.

"She's taken Marla into Bendigo to make a report at the police station. I guess they'll be a couple of hours."

Cassie envisaged Marla, her long slender thighs

barely covered by the indecently short shorts she'd worn at breakfast, occupying the passenger seat next to Blair. Appalled, she said, "Was that wise? I mean, this guy who's after Marla . . . he's got a gun. He was out at the Murphys' last night asking questions."

Her mother's expression was quizzical. "Blair's no fool. I'm sure they'll be just fine, Cassie." She unscrewed the top from her water bottle and took several deep swallows. "Blair mentioned she's moving into a new apartment soon," she said in the mild conversational tone she always used when she was soliciting information.

Cassie gave an unhelpful shrug. "It's down by the river."

"Sounds charming."

"I haven't seen it."

"Blair thought Marla could stay there until she sorts herself out."

Blair and Marla sharing an apartment with big soft beds and a romantic view across the city? Cassie fanned herself. The air seemed too thick to breathe.

"She said you weren't too keen on having Marla at Delia's place," her mother continued. "I must admit I'm surprised, Cassie. You've been quite rude to Marla. It's not like you at all."

Responding to the note of censure, Cassie said, "I didn't come out here to get tangled up in some other woman's domestic disaster. We've got enough problems of our own."

Beneath the shady brim of her hat, Faith Jensen's face registered her disquiet. "Is that the only reason you're angry?"

"What do you mean?"

"Blair seems to think you're feeling resentful because you haven't had enough time with me."

Cassie rolled her eyes. "So you sat around analyzing me while I wasn't here?"

"There's no need to be so defensive," her mother said. "Believe it or not, we both care about you, Cassie. Sweetheart, I'm worried about you. Are you really happy in Melbourne? You seem so —"

"I'm perfectly happy."

"You can come back if you're not. Forget about the money. We'll get through."

Cassie barely refrained from stamping her foot. "I wish you would listen to me. I'm fine. I don't need you to run my life."

"Cassie. I don't want to interfere. I —"

"Please, Mom." Sensing her mother's hurt, Cassie felt a rush of dismay. "Let's just leave it. I'm sorry I shouted." She stuffed her hands in her pocket and took a few paces back and forth. When she lifted her gaze from the parched earth, she was momentarily stunned at the grief on her mother's face.

"You're so much like your father," Faith Jensen said.

Cassie didn't know what to say. She put her arms around her mother, gently rubbing her back. Eventually, she said, "Sometimes I feel like he's right here."

Her mother released a slow breath, moisture softening the grooves around her eyes. "I feel that, too." Glancing to one side, she said lightly, "Could you send us some rain, James?"

Cassie gazed up at the cloudless sky. Moving away

from her mother, arms outstretched, head tilted back, she yelled, "If there's anyone listening, we'd like some rain. Please." Immediately, something wet landed on her face and she spun toward her mother.

Faith Jensen was standing with her thumb over the mouth of her water flask, shaking the bottle so that droplets of water flew up in the air and cascaded down. They evaporated almost before they reached the earth.

"Just practicing," she said.

Blair and Marla got back in the late afternoon. From the lawn, Cassie watched them get out of Blair's Landcruiser. They looked so companionable, she felt like hurling her magazine at them. Nudging away a fat white cockatoo which was determinedly shredding the cover, she stood up and waved.

"Mom's resting," she informed Blair in what she hoped was a normal sounding tone. "We've been down in the southern paddocks all afternoon."

Marla seemed interested in this. "How are those lambs faring today?"

"They all survived the night. Mom thinks they'll make it."

"You'll need to keep them on the bottle for another week or so," Marla said. "Most of the ewes won't come into milk again. They were too dehydrated."

Propped against the hood, her demeanor nonchalant, Blair said, "It's a lot of work for your mom, Cassie. Think she'll hold up okay?"

"I thought I'd come out again in a couple of weeks," Cassie said, covertly tracing the curve of Blair's breasts with quick darting glances.

Blair lifted an eyebrow and Cassie felt heat suffuse her cheeks.

"I'd love a cup of tea," Marla said in her polite English accent. "Do you mind if I help myself?"

"Go right ahead," Cassie invited. "Do you know where everything is?"

"I'm sure I can figure it out." With a brilliant smile at Blair, Marla excused herself and strolled off.

As soon as she was out of sight, Blair casually took one of Cassie's hands. Sliding her fingers between Cassie's, she drew her close and dropped a light kiss on her mouth. "Hi there."

Cassie felt winded, her gaze locked on the soft hollow at the base of Blair's throat. She could hardly believe she had kissed her there last night.

Blair seemed to read her thoughts. "It barely seems real does it?"

Cassie shook her head. One moment it felt completely impossible, the next it was all too real.

"Are you upset about what happened?" Blair asked.

Upset? Cassie was struck by the blandness of the word. Upset was when you missed the tram or locked yourself out of your apartment, or your cat messed on the carpet. It bore no resemblance to the turmoil she was experiencing. "I'm not sure how I feel," she said.

Blair's arms slipped around her. "Well, I feel great. And hey, I almost managed to look your mom in the eye this morning."

"Congratulations," Cassie said dryly. "I almost threw up my breakfast."

Leaning into one another, they shared laughter that was tinted with relief.

After a moment, Cassie said. "I wondered how it would be. You know the first time I ever did . . . that."

"You have to learn to say the word *sex*, Cassie." Blair pronounced 'sex' with sibilant emphasis. "Anyway, how was it for you? — as they say in those awful movies."

Cassie knew her cheeks were bright red. "It was um . . . fine." Another understatement. Squirming inside, she enquired, "How about you?"

"Well, I've never been one for conducting post-mortems the morning after . . . but since you ask . . ." She placed her mouth very close to Cassie's ear and whispered. "You were delicious. I wish I could drag you off right now and do it again."

Queasy with longing, Cassie turned her head, bringing her mouth to Blair's. As she extended the tip of her tongue, there was a clattering sound somewhere behind them.

Marla was standing on the veranda, holding a tray of snacks, her demeanor one of frozen astonishment.

Hurriedly, Cassie attempted to detach herself from Blair. But Blair caught her firmly by the hand. Leading her toward the veranda, she said, so that only Cassie could hear, "We don't have to explain ourselves to anyone, Cassie. We haven't done anything wrong."

That was all very well, Cassie thought. But

Marla's face spoke volumes. Her delicate hand shook as she poured tea from the battered silver pot Cassie could remember banging on the kitchen floor when she was too small to walk. Completely ignoring Cassie's presence, she eventually directed a sharp question at Blair. "Does Mrs. Jensen know about this?"

Blair looked completely unfazed. "I think that's between Cassie and her mother, don't you?"

Marla flushed a little, her gaze flicking from Blair to Cassie. "I'm sorry," she said abruptly. "It's no business of mine."

They sipped tea and crunched on crackers for a few minutes, distracted by the spectacle of a group of white cockatoos cavorting beneath the lawn spray.

One of the larger birds hopped across to the veranda steps and began a vitriolic tirade. Chiding him with small clucking sounds, Cassie took a handful of pumpkin seeds from the screw-top container her mother kept beneath the coffee table and flung them out across the lawn.

Marla began to laugh. "Did that bird say what I thought it said?" She mimicked a parrot voice. "'Where's the bloody seeds? Get up you lazy cow.'"

"He's an old friend," Cassie explained. "His name is Elvis. I found him as a fledgling and hand-reared him."

"You taught him to be rude and ungrateful?" Blair teased.

"Not entirely. He has a few party tricks." Cassie whistled and extended her arm. Somewhat reluctantly her pet alighted, his head cocked, dark eyes fixed on her. As she began humming, he fluffed out his feathers and croaked a unique and awful rendition of

"Love Me Tender". He then pecked Cassie lovingly on the cheek, executed the bobbing bow that was peculiar to his breed, and returned to his pumpkin seeds.

"I saw it with my own eyes, folks." Blair laughed. "The King is alive and well in the Australian outback."

CHAPTER THIRTEEN

Marla excused herself soon after dinner, saying she needed to get packed.

"Well, I'm going for a ride," Cassie said. "Anyone want to come?"

The invitation sounded half-hearted. Reluctant to intrude on what was obviously a leaving ritual of some kind, Blair shook her head.

"She used to go out with her dad," Faith said, watching her daughter leave the room.

"She's like him?"

"Very much so." Faith sipped the lemonade she had poured a little earlier. "It's quite uncanny at times — some of her mannerisms. And she's stubborn as hell, just like James."

"You seem pretty strong-willed yourself," Blair remarked.

Faith conceded with a slightly rueful smile. "I like to think it's coupled with common sense, but I suspect that has more to do with my age than my gene pool."

An image of Delia flashed through Blair's mind. A little guiltily she met Faith's eyes and both women laughed.

"You were thinking about my sister too? It's no wonder Cassie is so impetuous. I think it runs on both sides of the family." Faith's hazel eyes softened. "How did you meet Delia, anyway?"

Blair laughed. "Now, that's a story."

Delia had seen one of Blair's early attempts at a documentary and had contacted her, outraged over what she called glamorization of animal torture.

"It was about falconry," Blair explained. "I showed a couple of hunting birds catching prey."

"And Delia ordered you to withdraw it?"

"Uh-huh." Blair grinned. "She said my name would be mud. Decent people would be outraged."

Faith rolled her eyes. "What did you do?"

"I didn't withdraw it. But I offered to make another documentary on any animal issue she chose."

With a long-suffering air, Faith said, "Baby seals, right?"

"It was one of the smartest things I ever did," Blair said. "Made my reputation overnight."

Faith crossed to the sideboard and poured some more lemonade into their glasses. "Did you have strong feelings about the issue yourself?"

"Not at the time," Blair admitted. "To be honest, I didn't know much about conservation generally. Making that film changed the direction I was going in, careerwise."

Faith returned to her chair and handed Blair a glass. "So what are you filming over here — yet another marsupial movie?"

Blair shook her head. "It's funny you should ask. I've been working on a new project but I can't settle. I'm not sure why, exactly." She paused, attempting to unravel her feelings. "I feel like I'm at some kind of crossroads. I guess a relationship break-up unsettles you. I mean, you build up this picture of your future — at least I did."

Faith's gaze was very still. "And when the picture vanishes, you have to find something to put in the empty frame. Fast."

"That scares me too, I suppose." Blair swirled her lemonade around the ice cubes. "I don't want to rush into anything — make some stupid mistake because I don't know what I should be doing anymore."

Faith was silent for a moment, examining her weathered hands. "Farmer's hands," she commented eventually. "Not a pretty sight, are they?"

Blair touched the callused palm she extended. "My grandmother always used to say there's no shame in hard work."

"Protestant values." Faith sighed. "I feel that way myself. Only I'm not sure whether I can justify keeping this place any longer. It's taken so much from me. And I have so little left to give." She laughed abruptly. "I should look on the bright side. Thousands of women feel that way about their husbands, only they can't put them up for sale."

"Are you really thinking about selling Narrung?"

"I ask myself that question nearly every day," Faith replied. "Right now I'm holding on for Cassie's sake more than my own. She's terribly attached to the place. I think it's the most important link she has with her father."

You don't get over it, Blair found herself thinking. Time goes by. Life happens. You just have to deal with it. Cassie's father was such a powerful presence at Narrung, it was possible to believe he was only temporarily away.

"You were with your partner a long time, weren't you?" Faith broke in on Blair's thoughts.

Blair felt her throat constrict. "We were together twenty years."

"Was that why you came to Australia? To make a clean break?"

"It was a factor," Blair responded. She'd thought long and hard about her motives before she'd booked her travel. "I didn't run away exactly. I wanted a change."

"And New York in winter . . ." Faith's tone was light, shifting their conversation to safer ground.

Appreciating her sensitivity, Blair nodded in agreement. "It's not an easy city at any time of the year, but winter is the pits. It was sure a relief to get here."

"We're warm most of the year," Faith said. "Except for summer, when we're plain boiling."

"It must be hell working the property in that heat. We were only out for a few hours today and I felt exhausted."

"Narrung covers five hundred square miles," Faith said. "There are much bigger spreads, especially in South Australia. But this place is quite enough to manage."

"Faith —" In the back of Blair's mind, the germ of an idea had taken root. "This part of the state . . ." she began. "Does it get a lot of visitors?"

"You mean tourists?" Faith shook her head. "If you're thinking about some kind of country bed and breakfast concept, I looked into that a while back. There's not enough in these parts for guests to do. Besides, Narrung is too run down, and I have no capital to put into it."

Blair was silent. That wasn't quite what she had in mind. But her idea was so poorly formed, it wasn't worth discussing yet. She would have to think some more about it. Besides, it wasn't her place to start telling another woman how to run her life.

Faith stood, casting a glance toward the window. "I believe that's Cassie I can hear. I'm going to make some hot chocolate. Would you like a cup, Blair?"

Blair shook her head, sensing that Faith might appreciate some time alone with her daughter. "I think I'll take a shower and turn in for the night."

"It was good talking with you, Blair." Faith paused in the doorway. "You know, you're very welcome here at Narrung, whether you're with Cassie or not."

For a moment Blair was tempted to read

something into the comment. Was Faith saying she had guessed? Blair shot a brief glance at her. "That's very kind of you."

Faith's gaze was unwavering. "I like you, Blair," she said.

It was very late when Cassie crept into the bedroom. Unable to detect Blair's breathing, she approached her bed on tiptoe.

"It's okay," Blair said. "I'm awake."

Cassie perched on the edge of the bed, her heart thudding. She could smell Blair's faint clean scent.

"You must be tired," Blair said. "It's late."

Was that Blair's polite way of saying she didn't feel like company? Cassie stretched a hand into the darkness, found Blair's face and traced a path to her ear, fingering the delicate contours her mouth remembered from the night before. "I know it's late but I'm wide awake," she murmured.

Blair arrested her hand. "So, will you get into bed with me?"

Cassie pulled back the curtains, flooding the room with bright moonlight. Blair had thrown back the bedclothes and lay naked, propped on an elbow. Her body was compact and streamlined, a sharp contrast to the fullness of Cassie's.

Delighting in the difference, Cassie removed her nightshirt and slid into Blair's arms as if she belonged there. Her skin goosebumped. Everything felt so new, she couldn't stop shivering.

Blair drew her close. "God." She sighed against Cassie's lips. "I've been desperate to kiss you all day."

Cassie opened her mouth to reply but Blair licked the words away, murmuring, "Sssh."

Returning Blair's kisses, Cassie pressed herself closer, until their breasts were crushed and their legs tangled. Blair stroked her, kissed her throat. Her caresses felt far too leisurely and gentle. Squirming, Cassie whispered, "Blair —"

Blair hesitated, her mouth poised above one of Cassie's nipples. "Mmm?"

Cassie touched her hair, remembering the brush of it between her thighs the previous night. "I want you so much."

Blair laughed softly, altering her position so that she was lying on top of Cassie. "And you can have me."

Loving the feel of her weight, Cassie parted her legs, locking them around Blair. Kissing her hard, she murmured, "You're teasing me."

"I'm turning you on," Blair corrected. "See . . ." She slid a hand back and forth between Cassie's thighs, then withdrew it, trailing slippery fingers past Cassie's mouth to her own.

Cassie caught her wrist, pulling her roughly down. They rolled against each other, licking and kissing and biting, until Cassie was wet with sweat and longing. Panting, she turned onto her stomach, Blair's arm trapped beneath her. Her throat felt dry and choked with desire, her tongue too thick for words.

"I want to get inside you," Blair whispered in her ear, her nipples hard against Cassie's back.

Cassie could manage only a small moan as Blair

drew her upright. Turning to face Blair, she linked her hands behind Blair's neck, offering kiss for kiss. By the time Blair found her clitoris and set about creating the tiny exquisite explosions she craved, Cassie's limbs felt so heavy she could not remain upright.

She did not resist as Blair lowered her onto the cool sheets. Overwhelmed with sensation, she gripped Blair's shoulders. If sex were color, she thought, theirs would be more purple than the mountains, greener than grass, whiter than light.

Some time later, encircled by Blair's arms, she stared out at the big orange moon and promised herself she would always remember that moment. For, as she watched a star plummet to earth, she knew she was in love.

CHAPTER FOURTEEN

"There's a message for you on the answering machine," Blair told Cassie as she emerged from her room after unpacking. "Someone called Antoinette."

Cassie took the scrap of paper she held out, her heart leaping slightly as their hands brushed.

"It's a pity you have to go to work tonight," Marla commented from the beanbag in the sitting room.

She didn't sound too broken up about it, Cassie thought cynically. "I don't mind," she said. "It's been nice to get away for a few days." She carried the phone out into the hallway and dialed Beauties.

Antoinette answered. Jude was sick, she explained. Could Cassie work a few extra hours to help Nan out?

"You mean on the fantasm line?" Cassie was already shaking her head.

"No, no." Antoinette gave a throaty laugh. "Nan will handle the calls. But it would be a help if you could log times for her."

"Okay. Sure." She could definitely live without Marla Farrant's company for the rest of the day, she decided. It was ridiculous for her to be so jealous, of course. Blair wasn't interested in the vet. "What time do you want me?" she asked Antoinette.

"As soon as you can make it, angel. Oh, and by the way," Antoinette added. "It's double rate for overtime."

Cassie checked her watch and returned to the living room. "I have to go to work early," she said. "One of the others is sick and I'm filling in for her."

Blair frowned slightly. "But it's only five o'clock. You're not planning to work a twelve-hour shift, are you?"

"I'll take a tea break." Cassie gathered up her handbag and checked that she had the plastic pass card that gave her after-hours access to the building.

Blair picked her car keys up off the table. "I'll give you a lift."

Cassie shook her head. "It's okay. I can get a tram."

"I don't mind staying here alone," Marla offered, apparently under the impression that Cassie was making sacrifices on her behalf.

Cassie managed a polite smile. "There's no need. Honestly. I'll see you both in the morning." She headed for the door, avoiding Blair's piercing gaze.

"Cassie. Hold on a minute." Blair followed her into the hallway, her frustration evident.

"I've already said —"

"I know what you've said." Blair seemed to be forcing calm into her voice. "And I know you're determined to be independent. But you don't have to prove anything. I *want* to drive you to work. What's wrong with that?"

Cassie shrugged, trying to picture the building in St. Kilda Road. As far as she could recall there were no outward indications of Beauties' presence. "Okay," she conceded. "I'm sorry. It's really nice of you to offer. I just don't want to be a burden."

Blair rolled her eyes. "I'm not your guardian, Cassie."

"What are you?" The words were out before Cassie could prevent them. Looking at Blair, she detected a flicker of uncertainty which stabbed at her heart.

"I think it's too soon to ask that question." Blair locked the apartment door, and taking Cassie's hand in a determined grasp, escorted her to the ancient elevator.

They rode down in silence. Once in the lobby, Blair added, "I'm not trying to be evasive, Cassie. I'm just saying a lot has happened. We need some time to take it all in."

"You need time," Cassie observed softly.

Blair's stare was level. "Yes, I do."

* * * * *

144

Cassie felt as if she had chalk in her mouth. She and Blair barely spoke as they drove through the city.

"I'll pick you up," Blair offered as she drew up alongside the building. "What time do you get off?"

Cassie tried to seem grateful, instead of defensive. "A silly time," she said. "You'll still be in bed. I really don't mind taking a cab."

Blair's mouth thinned. "I don't know why you're making this so hard. Do you think I'm trying to take control of you, or something?"

Cassie shook her head. A car tooted them from behind. "We're holding up traffic."

"We're bigger than he is," Blair said. "Call me when you're finished. I'll come and get you."

"No. I —"

"Cassie. Please. I don't like you riding across town in cabs while it's dark. Your mom feels that way too —"

Cassie felt a flare of anger. "Well, both of you better get used to it. I'm twenty in a few weeks' time. I'm not a baby any more. I —"

Blair raised her voice. "A woman was murdered by a taxi driver just last month."

The tooting behind them got more insistent.

"Look, I have to go." Cassie swung open her door. "Let's talk about this another time."

"I'll be waiting here at five," Blair said flatly. "We can talk then."

Cassie was shaking so much she could hardly get the office door open.

"Sweetie," Antoinette's smile collapsed. "What happened?"

"Nothing," Cassie said.

Antoinette raised a thin reddish-brown eyebrow. "And I had breakfast with the Pope."

Cassie flopped onto an easy chair. "I'll be fine. I'm just tired from the weekend."

Antoinette nodded slowly, dense eyelashes concealing her expression. "And how is your mother?"

"She's fine."

"That's not the problem, then?" Antoinette stood, smoothed her skirt and, on immensely high heels, wobbled her way to the cappuccino machine. "Are you in love?"

Cassie could actually feel her jaw dropping.

"I thought so." Antoinette poured foaming milk into a cup. "Who is she?"

"What makes you think it's a woman?" Cassie inquired weakly. Surely she didn't have it written all over her face.

Antoinette shrugged. "Well, it is, isn't it? I have an instinct for these things, dear."

Cassie sipped the coffee she was handed. "We had a fight," she said gloomily. "No one knows I work here."

"You don't want *her* to find out?" Antoinette patted the stiff curls clustered around her cheeks.

"Not yet. I mean . . . it's complicated."

"It's always complicated when you lead a double life, sweetie, let me tell you." Antoinette heaved an exaggerated sigh. "Take some free advice. Tell her before she finds out for herself."

"I don't know what she'll think." Cassie worried out loud.

146

"All the more reason to tell her," Antoinette advised. "And remember. You're a receptionist. You just answer the phones."

If only it were that simple, Cassie thought.

Blair installed Marla in the Southgate apartment early that evening, confident she would be safe there. With their guest out of the way, perhaps she and Cassie could have the discussion they clearly needed.

She had overreacted around Cassie's desire for independence, Blair realized. They had only slept together twice and already she was feeling desperately possessive. Or was it insecurity?

Leaving her car parked beneath the apartment, Blair meandered along Southgate Boulevard. The Yarra looked beautiful, shimmering with reflected city lights. Dozens of people were out strolling, some with small white dogs wearing tartan caps. It was so clean, Blair marveled. No litter, no grime, no taxis honking, no homeless huddled on benches.

Music from nearby cafés drifted on the faint breeze. Bejeweled women on dainty heels picked their way across the cobblestones, headed for the opera, and from St. Kilda Road came the clip-clop of horse-drawn carriages, a common sight on the city streets.

Blair took the steps up past the concert halls to the leafy avenue between the Victorian Arts Center and Queen Victoria Gardens. It was an inspiring walk, tiny yellow lights adorning the trees, fountains playing, The Angel, an enormous mosaic creature of a thousand faces, gazing down on passers-by.

Thousands of birds relentlessly circled the tall metal dome — Melbourne's answer to the Eiffel Tower — which capped the Arts Center. The din was astounding. Covering her ears, Blair paused at a billboard for *Angels in America*. She wondered if Cassie enjoyed theater — if she'd ever been to a play. She was so young, Blair thought. Too young.

Feeling despondent all of a sudden, she headed back toward Southgate. She had made a mistake, she decided. Narrung had felt like another world. It had been all too easy to surrender to the heat and thrill of the moment, ignoring the prickles of doubt, assigning the consequences of their lovemaking to some nebulous far-off future.

Blair drove home planning what she was going to say to Cassie and trying to imagine what the young woman was thinking. Obviously she resented the attempts of older people to curtail her new-found freedom. Blair could remember herself at twenty — full of arrogant assumptions about how much she knew. Cassie was less arrogant, but also much less sophisticated.

Pouring herself a shot of brandy, Blair sat at the dining table and tried to distract herself by going over her documentary budget once more. Two hundred thousand dollars. It struck her suddenly that such an appalling amount could be spent on one hour of television entertainment, no matter how educational.

She cradled her head in her hands. Nothing about the project really excited her. According to the world in general, Blair Carroll was the woman who made those great wildlife documentaries. That was her identity, in a nutshell. But she felt supremely stale, as if she were simply going through the motions.

People often said they envied her having such clear direction in her life, a real sense of purpose. Blair poured a second shot of brandy and, nursing it, paced restlessly into the hallway, trying to connect with that long-held feeling of confidence in her future. Cassie's bedroom door was open. For a moment she hovered outside, tempted to go in, but uncertain why she should want to.

Turning away, she paused, her attention caught by a small scrap of paper on the floor. She picked it up, reading her own handwriting. It was the telephone message she had given to Cassie earlier that evening. "Antoinette" was her boss, Blair supposed.

She glanced toward the telephone, and on an impulse picked it up and dialed the number shown. Cassie answered.

"Good evening. Beauties Limited. This is Cindy. How may we be of service?"

Cindy? Blair replaced the receiver, her mouth dry.

Cassie dropped the phone into its cradle. "I hate that," she said. "The ones who hang up without saying anything."

"They get off on your voice," Nan said. "Cheapskates. They can hear all they want on the fantasm line for three bucks a minute."

"How much do you get paid for each call?" Cassie asked, marking up the log. So far that evening Nan had clocked over a hundred and thirty minutes. She'd kept one guy on the line for nearly a quarter of an hour.

"Antoinette's generous. We get a dollar a minute plus she pays our health insurance. Why, are you thinking about it?"

Cassie shook her head vigorously. "I couldn't possibly . . ."

"You'd be surprised," Nan said. "I thought I'd never be able to do it, but Jude showed me her book and bingo. I doubled my pay." She opened a desk drawer and pulled out a battered red journal, instructing Cassie, "Take a look."

Cassie scanned the well-thumbed pages. Jude had scripted literally dozens of sexual fantasies, complete with oohs and aahs. Cassie read a few lines of one titled "Phone Box." "I can't believe anyone gets turned on by this stuff," she said.

"I sure don't." Nan stubbed out a cigarette. "It probably helps my job that I'm a dyke."

"In what way?"

"Well they just don't mean anything at all, and they don't affect my relationship. They're men's fantasies, not mine." She lifted the phone, teasingly offering it to Cassie who backed off hastily and made a show of logging the time.

Nan was an expert, she thought, listening to her companion draw the call out with a combination of taunting comments and panting sounds. Between false gasps, Nan pointed toward the biscuit barrel, making eating gestures. Cassie fished out a couple of her favorite chocolate slices and handed them over.

When the escort line rang again, she picked it up. Only this time, before she could say a word, a voice said, "Cassie?" and Blair informed her harshly, "Be outside in ten minutes time. I'm picking you up."

"You can't be serious," Nan said. "What makes her think she can order you around. What's her problem, anyway?"

"She doesn't know about Beauties. Well, she didn't..."

"But she does now, and she thinks she can tell you how to run your life. Tell her to get lost. She's some friend of your aunt's. So what?"

Cassie stared miserably at the floor. "It's worse than that. She...we..."

"You haven't?" Nan lifted a ringing phone and set it down again, her bright blue eyes gleaming. "Cassie. You're on with this woman?"

"I don't know," Cassie mumbled. "We slept together on the weekend, but since then she's been acting really strangely."

"Cold feet," Nan speculated. "She's a lot older than you, huh?"

"I'm not pressuring her about anything," Cassie said. "It's all been so sudden."

"But you're pretty keen on her, right?"

"Right. I —"

"You're serious?"

Cassie nodded. She felt utterly depressed. "I was going to tell her everything tonight."

"Mmm." Nan's small face was creased with concentration. "This calls for a plan."

"Or a gun," Cassie muttered. "I may as well shoot myself."

CHAPTER FIFTEEN

Cassie was not standing outside the building, as she'd been instructed. Furious, Blair slammed the car door and stalked up to the main entrance, peering into the marble foyer. There was no security guard in evidence and no sign of Cassie.

Just as she was digging around for her mobile phone, a small blond woman appeared at the doors, apparently leaving the building.

Blair detained her politely. "Excuse me, do you know of a business in this building known as Beauties?"

"Sure." The blond stopped chewing her gum for a moment. "It's on the ninth floor."

"I need to see someone there urgently. I wonder if you'd mind letting me in."

The woman hesitated. "It's really not within our security regulations. You'll have to sign the visitors' book."

"That's just fine." Blair followed her through the security door and into the foyer, where she initialed a leather-bound volume chained to the reception desk.

"Is she expecting you?" the blond asked.

"She was supposed to meet me outside, but she didn't show."

"Then I'll take you up," she offered obligingly. "You have to use a pass card to ride in the elevator."

The woman gave her a slow once-over as they rode up. Terrific, Blair thought. She was being cruised by a reasonably attractive woman and she was so stressed it didn't even raise her pulse.

As the bell signaled the ninth floor, she did her best to produce a smile. "Thanks. I really appreciate this."

"No problem." The blond pressed the descend button and the doors closed on what looked very much like a wink.

Slightly disconcerted, Blair entered a pastel office suite with Beauties scripted in gold lettering everywhere she looked. There was a small crystal bell sitting on the reception desk. She rang this sharply. After a minute, when no one came, she followed the faint sound of talking and pushed open an office door.

Cassie was sitting at a desk, on the telephone. "Very well, sir," she said as Blair approached. "Tania will call on you at one-thirty. Thank you for choosing Beauties." As she returned the phone to it's cradle, Blair caught her hand.

"What do you think you're doing?"

White-faced, Cassie stared. "I'm working. Do you mind?"

"Tell me this is not what I think it is." Blair gazed around the room. Tasteful, if a little clichéd. Obviously a high-class joint.

"I don't have to tell you anything." Cassie's mouth trembled. "This is my job. I'm a receptionist. I take bookings and write them down. I tell our staff where they're going. That's all."

"And your name is Cindy?"

Cassie flushed. "I'm hardly going to give my real name."

Blair shoved her hands into her pockets. The palms felt damp. "Have you told your mom about this?"

"Don't bring her into it."

"I know you're doing this to help her out, but I'm sure she would be upset if she knew . . ."

"Are you going to tell her?" Cassie asked coldly.

"I don't know. That depends."

"On what?"

"On whether you come home with me now and give in your notice," Blair snapped.

The phone started ringing. Ignoring it, Cassie moved out from behind the desk, her eyes electric blue with anger. "I don't know what gives you the right to come here and boss me around," she blazed. "But I'm not leaving."

"Cassie, I don't think you know what you're

154

getting involved in. This is prostitution. It means women being bought and sold like cattle."

"No one is forcing anyone to work," Cassie said in a distant voice. "Our escorts are well looked after."

"Listen to you!" Blair suppressed an urge to grab her shoulders and shake her. "You've been completely brainwashed."

"That's not true!" Cassie objected. "It's not up to me to judge other women. I just do my job."

Blair detected a waver of uncertainty. "Don't tell me you haven't thought about the ethics of what you're doing?"

Cassie's eyes shone. "Of course I have. How dumb do you think I am?"

The phone finally stopped ringing. Before it could start again, Blair took it off the hook. She ached to pull Cassie close, reassure her that everything would be all right with her beloved Narrung. "I think you're very loyal and very brave. But you can't save the farm by working here."

Cassie gave her a withering look. "What do you suggest — washing dishes for three bucks an hour? I like it here. I get treated well." She hesitated. "Surely you're the last person who should be telling me what to do."

"What do you mean?"

"You're a lesbian having sex with someone half your age. Some people would think that was just as wicked as prostitutes or phone sex."

Blair's stomach churned. "It's not the same thing at all, and you know it."

"It is too," Cassie insisted. "It's about choice.

Look, I know there are places that exploit women. But Beauties doesn't support pimping, or paying off the cops, or —"

"Enough." Blair could hardly bear to have this conversation. Nineteen years undefiled by urban sleaziness, and it had only taken a few weeks for Cassie to lose her innocence.

It was as if Cassie had guessed her thoughts. "Don't look at me like that." She tilted her chin stubbornly. "I haven't changed. I just know more."

I don't want you knowing *this,* Blair thought. "You could work for me," she said without thinking. "I need an assistant. It won't pay a lot, but you'd be in an industry with long term prospects."

Cassie was already shaking her head. " I don't know anything about making films."

"You could learn." Blair paused, suddenly perplexed by the strength of her feelings. In the past, Lisa had attempted to engage her in endless debate on anti-pornography issues, but Blair had refused. Conservation was her thing, she always said. Certainly she was a feminist, but somehow the daily extinction of several species disturbed her more than the existence of the sex industry.

She studied Cassie. Flushed with indignation, black curls flopping waywardly into her eyes, she was beautiful. *I feel powerless,* Blair realized with shocking clarity. She was overwhelmingly attracted to Cassie and the feelings had brought up all her insecurities.

"Cassie —" she began, then glanced up sharply at the sound of a knock.

The blond women who had let her into the building was standing in the doorway, calmly chewing gum. "I got an extra burger, Cassie," she said. "Do you want it?"

Shaking her head, Cassie performed the introductions, explaining, "Nan works with me."

"I do phone fantasies," Nan said with a trace of challenge. "Can I get anyone coffee?"

Blair caught a look that passed between Cassie and her workmate. "Not for me. I was just leaving."

"Why don't you go home, Cass," Nan said. "The rush is over. I can manage on my own till five."

Cassie seemed hesitant. "If you're sure."

"I won't tell Antoinette. Go on." Nan made a shooing gesture. "You both look awful. Fighting is hell, huh?"

* * * * *

Cassie soaped herself automatically. Her body felt tender, muscles aching in unexpected places, her skin overly sensitive, as though it had been exposed to an excess of sun and weather. Relieved she had taken the night off work, she turned her face into the shower and heaved a dry sob.

She wanted to cry but tears wouldn't come. Part of her was angry with Blair, another part was simply in love. She wanted Blair to hold her and shut out the rest of the world. They should have talked that morning. But instead, Blair had gone off in the Landcruiser, saying she needed some time to think.

Cassie turned off the shower and dried herself. The towel felt rough, like the back of her throat. Dusting talc over her breasts and thighs, she buttoned a fresh nightshirt to the neck. She didn't know how to face Blair, what she could possibly say. They hadn't spoken to each other on the way home that morning, except when Blair mentioned that she had given Marla the use of her new apartment for a few days so that she could finalize her plans to leave Melbourne.

Cassie brushed her teeth. Her jaw ached too — probably from clamping it shut so that she didn't shout at Blair. A surge of anger shook her again. She could understand Blair's distaste for the industry she was working in, but she was offended by what felt like emotional blackmail.

What made Blair think she had the right to dictate to her? Did having sex mean she was owned by someone? They hadn't talked about that either. In fact, since they had started having sex, most of their communication had been disastrous. It was better when they were just friends, Cassie thought miserably. Maybe they should have stayed that way.

Blair tried to concentrate on getting to sleep, but she was acutely aware of Cassie's presence in the opposite bedroom. She was awake. That much was obvious from her restless stirring and periodic forays to the refrigerator.

The heat didn't help. It was one of Melbourne's infamous sticky nights — airless, unbearably humid, storms threatening somewhere on the city's perimeters. Hearing Cassie get up again, Blair switched on her light and, separating damp sheet from her legs, swung her feet to the floor.

It was nearly four in the morning. In an hour or

so the birds would start welcoming the new day. Groaning, Blair slid into her robe and padded out to the kitchen.

Cassie glanced up from her inspection of the fridge, her expression combining guilt and defiance. In one hand, she had a large bowl of ice cream, in the other a packet of chocolate biscuits. Comfort food.

"That looks good." Blair remarked, her gaze drawn to the tug of Cassie's nightshirt across her breasts. "Any chance I could share?"

Cassie's eyes widened slightly. "Get yourself a spoon."

Blair opened the cutlery drawer, and extracted a dessert spoon. "We could sit in my bed and listen to the Mamas and the Papas," she suggested blandly.

Cassie's mouth twitched into an involuntary smile. "Sound's groovy." She closed the fridge and trailed after Blair, asking, "Is there really a Mamas and Papas record?"

"Your aunt has everything. The Doors, Sonny and Cher, Steppenwolf, Bob Dylan, The Electric Prunes."

Cassie placed her ice cream on the headboard and climbed onto the bed. "The only thing missing in this pad is the mirrors on the ceiling."

Blair laughed, relieved as much as she was amused. Sitting on the bed beside Cassie, she touched her shoulder very lightly, then cupped her cheeks and placed a single lingering kiss on her mouth. "I'm sorry," she whispered.

Cassie leaned into her. "I'm sorry too. I wish I'd told you sooner . . . about everything."

"I wish I hadn't reacted so badly when I found out," Blair said, weaving her fingers into Cassie's soft curls. "I behaved like a jerk."

Cassie's gaze was very candid. "What's happening with us, Blair?"

"I don't know," Blair said with difficulty. "I care about you, Cassie. But I'm having a hard time with my emotions in general."

"You don't want a relationship with me?"

"I don't think I can. I'm afraid I'd short-change you."

Cassie ate a spoonful of ice cream. "I want a relationship with you."

Taken aback at her directness, Blair said, "I don't want to write off that possibility. But the timing is all wrong. You're very young — just starting out. I have a mountain of baggage from my last relationship."

Cassie didn't seem impressed with Blair's reasoning. "But how do you actually feel about me?"

Blair gave the question some room. Lust was the first thing that sprang to mind, followed by tenderness, a growing yearning for Cassie's company. "I care about you," she said, adding cautiously, "I'd like for us to spend more time together."

"As lovers?"

"I'm the first person you've had sex with." Blair took a spoonful of ice cream. It was like swallowing a golf ball. "I don't want to tie you into anything."

"You mean, *you* don't want to feel tied." Cassie observed flatly.

Blair stopped short of making an automatic denial. Cassie was right. She wasn't ready to enter into any kind of commitment. Releasing a pent-up breath, she said, "I'm sorry, Cassie. I really think we should give it some time."

Cassie handed Blair the bowl of ice cream, saying,

"You can have the rest." Rolling onto her stomach, she propped her chin on her arms, her thin nightshirt settling into the hollow of her back.

Blair placed the remaining ice cream uneaten on the headboard, telling herself it was for the best. Even if she did want a relationship with Cassie, it would be unfair, maybe even unethical. She allowed herself to look for a moment on the curve of Cassie's bottom, remembering the feel of her, the unself-conscious pleasure she took in her body.

Intense blue eyes met hers. "So, you think I should get some more experience?" Cassie said. "Experiment a little?"

Blair's mouth dried. She found Cassie's frank appraisal very disturbing. Her skin prickled as though being touched. "That's up to you," she responded evasively.

"Does sex always change everything?" Cassie shifted onto her side to face Blair.

"I don't think I can answer that," Blair said. "I've only had three lovers in my life. The first two were all about coming to terms with my identity. Then I met Lisa."

Cassie lowered her eyes, her expression veiled. "Are you still in love with her?"

Blair pictured Lisa's oval face, the slightly sharp nose she complained about, her fine light brown eyes, often narrowed with concentration. She waited for the customary hollowness in her gut, the rush of emotion — pain, anger, self-blame.

Instead, her mind strayed to a holiday they had taken in Denver two years ago. They played, relaxed, walked in the snow, but did not make love at all. Later, they had talked about that and concluded that their relationship was more to do with deep friendship than passion.

Blair remembered the sense of sadness she had suppressed back then, the troubled resignation that arose every time she contemplated a limitless future with a woman whom she no longer saw as a lover. Lisa had been right to finish their relationship, she thought with a shock of realization. Perhaps their friendship could survive the change in circumstance, after all.

Blair slid down the bed resting her face on the pillow next to Cassie's. "You know, for an old lady of thirty-eight, I have a lot to learn. I'm not in love with Lisa. I haven't been in love with her for a long time."

Cassie lifted a finger to Blair's mouth, slowly tracing the line of her lips. "I know you're not in love with me," she said. "But we can still have fun, can't we? I could experiment — with you."

"Are you proposing we have sex and don't get married?" Blair captured Cassie's finger between her teeth and bit down slightly.

Cassie's stare was unblinking. "Can you cope?"

Blair could feel moisture building between her thighs. Releasing Cassie's finger, she kissed her hard on the mouth. It was going to be hell, she thought. And then some. "I think I'm woman enough," she said, pinning Cassie beneath her.

"Hey, not so fast!" Cassie wriggled out. "I thought this was my experiment."

Blair laughed softly. "I see." She twirled one of Cassie's curls around her little finger. "So, what are you going to do about it?"

Cassie blushed. "I . . ." Blair's expectant expression

made her feel weak and jittery. She placed a finger over the dark mole on Blair's shoulder, astonished that she could touch another person this way. Blair's skin felt different from her own, cooler somehow. It's color was golden against the pale olive of Cassie's. She smelled like wheat on a hot day. She tasted like apples.

I love you, Cassie thought.

"Mmm . . . I like that," Blair murmured, making Cassie suddenly aware . of what her fingers were doing — delicately exploring every inch of Blair's breasts and stomach.

"What else do you like?" Immediately, Cassie felt embarrassed for asking. A silly phrase from a satirical calendar on the wall at work leapt inappropriately into her mind — *Your body is an open book to me, baby.* She swallowed a mortified whimper.

"It's okay. You can ask." Blair stroked and kissed Cassie's face. Her mouth felt hot and firm, and increasingly passionate. With a sigh, she rolled onto her back, inviting Cassie into her arms.

The sensation of having a woman lying beneath her, was novel and deliciously shocking. Cassie's breasts fell heavily against Blair's. Her nipples were tight and her thigh felt wet, sandwiched between Blair's legs. Rocking back and forth, Cassie increased her pressure on the hidden source of the moisture.

"That feels good." Blair said.

"Am I too heavy?"

"I'll let you know if I can't breathe." Blair cupped and squeezed Cassie's breasts, then lifted her head to bite on a nipple.

The tugging sensation was exquisite, but completely unnerving. Abruptly losing her rhythm,

Cassie lurched forward, her breasts burying Blair's face. She tried to pull back, but Blair held her close and with a teasing laugh, said, "Let's try that some other time."

Cassie felt hopelessly inept. Last time, she had nearly bitten Blair's clitoris off and this time she'd tried to smother her. What was left — drowning her with her juices? "I'm sorry," she said.

Blair placed a finger over her lips. "Don't worry. We've got plenty of time to get used to each other."

Mentally repeating the phrase "plenty of time", Cassie nestled closer. "I want to make you happy."

Blair smoothed the curls back from her face. "I'm going to enjoy showing you exactly how to do that. Let's start with this." Taking Cassie's hand she placed it firmly on her soaking mound, adding, "See what you do to me."

Cassie's skin goosebumped. Working her fingers through the slippery tangle she dabbled in the luscious folds within. After a few moments, Blair took a sharp breath and guided Cassie's middle finger back and forth in a sensuous caress.

"Don't stop," she whispered when Cassie altered her pressure. "That's perfect." Color suffused her cheeks and advanced down her throat to her breasts and wrinkled nipples. Her breathing sounded harsh and shaky.

Around Cassie's finger the flesh grew swollen. She pressed a fraction harder, remembering her own cravings when Blair did this to her. With a moan of pleasure, Blair drew her down into a hungry kiss, her body communicating its yearnings so clearly Cassie had no room for doubt. Closing her eyes, she responded instinctively to each unspoken cue as if she were melting into Blair, their skin dissolving.

She grew conscious of a change in Blair's breathing, of her heart beating faster, then quite suddenly Blair clutched her hand, her thighs closing tightly together. In consternation, Cassie attempted to withdraw, fearing she had done something wrong.

To compound her dismay, Blair started to laugh and releasing Cassie's hand, drew her into a damp embrace. Kissing her languidly, she said, "Baby, that was great."

Bemused, Cassie stared at her. Eyes closed, skin flushed, she looked profoundly contented. *I did it,* Cassie marveled. Feeling decidedly smug, she pulled up the bedclothes and nestled against Blair, whispering in her ear, "Can we try that experiment again later?"

Blair laughed sleepily. "I don't see why not."

CHAPTER SIXTEEN

Delia Grace wheeled her luggage alongside the inspection counter where a Melbourne Airport customs officer stood waiting. It was typical, she thought. All the white-collar types went straight through, but she, in her faded muslin shirt and jeans, was singled out for a full search.

The officer, who seemed too young to have a paunchy stomach hanging over his belt, said it was random.

Oh sure, Delia felt like saying. There were

probably much more sinister reasons than her appearance which could account for government officials detaining her. She had a record of arrests and even a deportation. No doubt there was a big red spot on her computer file.

The paunchy officer signaled the dog handler, a stocky woman with bright red hair tied in an unbecoming ponytail.

Escorting her charge — a cheerful beagle — to the counter, the woman instructed blandly, "Would you mind opening your luggage, ma'am."

"You won't find any illegal substances." Delia unfastened the small padlocks that secured her three suitcases. "Just prescription drugs. I've listed them for you on the declaration."

The paunchy officer was examining Delia's declaration as though it were almost certainly a forgery. "Are you carrying anything for any other person?" he inquired.

"No."

The dog handler relaxed the collar on her beagle, which immediately homed in on Delia's cabin bag, wagging its tail and slobbering enthusiastically.

"Must be after my sanitary towels," Delia commented blithely. "I use recyclable cotton. I think the smell of blood kind of hangs around. You know what I mean?"

"She'd go for blood, all right." Touching the beagle lightly on the shoulder, the handler cooed, "Is that what you can smell, girl?"

Red faced, the paunchy officer said, "Do you have any foodstuffs amongst your possessions?"

"I've declared everything," Delia reiterated. "Tell me, how is it that I was selected for a search?"

"It's completely random, ma'am," he assured her. "We don't wish to cause inconvenience." He removed clothing from her largest case and laid it out on the counter.

"Be careful," Delia said. "My sex toys are in there somewhere." She slid a hand inside her case. "Here they are. My Pearlbird and my favorite butt plug. You should probably cavity-search for those. Just in case."

The officer seemed strangely reluctant to take the toys from her so Delia laid them out on the counter, where milling passengers could admire them.

"The Pearlbird is particularly good," she told the dog handler. "Why lie there frustrated, listening to him snore. That's what I always say. Just look at this."

She turned the vibrator on. The dog handler seemed genuinely interested and signaled another woman standing at the opposite wall.

Their male colleague hurriedly replaced Delia's clothing and returned her largest case to the luggage trolley. He then reached inside the smaller case and rummaged perfunctorily. A bead of sweat rolled past his temple and dripped onto his shirt.

"I wouldn't be without this," Delia informed the dog handler and her friend, as she made the insertable part of the vibrator writhe and squirm. "Can you imagine how that feels?"

"Well, I think that's all, thank you, ma'am." The male officer scribbled something on a sheet of paper and handed it to Delia, instructing, "Just hand that in as you pass through the exit."

"Why, thank you," Delia said politely. "Have a nice day."

As she walked away, he came after her. "Ma'am?" He pointed toward the counter. "You left something behind."

A small butt plug stood upright on an expanse of black vinyl.

"Why don't you keep that, Officer," Delia said sweetly. "You look like you could use a good time."

Half an hour later, Delia unlocked the door to her apartment and dragged her luggage inside. The place looked homely, she thought, kicking off her canvas shoes. A vase of flowers decorated the dining table and stacked on the sinkbench were a few unwashed dishes.

Blair would be working, she supposed, heading down the hallway to her bedroom. And Cassie — perhaps she was here too. Delia had only opened Faith's letter a week ago, after returning from a biotechnology conference in Brussels.

Yawning, she pushed open the door to her bedroom and froze. There, in a tangle of sheets, sound asleep in each other's arms, lay her best friend and her niece — naked as day.

Delia did the only thing she could. She telephoned her sister.

* * * * *

Blair woke with a faint start, imagining she could hear someone speaking. Bemused, she eased herself out of Cassie's embrace and slipped on her robe. There was definitely something. A voice.

"Oh, shit," she muttered, shaken by a jolt of recognition. "Oh, no."

With a distracted glance at Cassie, she hurried down the hallway and flung open the sitting-room door. Sprawled on the beanbag, Delia held the phone in one hand, a raw carrot in the other. Spotting Blair, she promptly threw the carrot at her.

"She's right here," Delia informed the person at the other end of the line. "Yes, I'll do that. 'Bye, darling." Dropping the receiver on the hook, she cast a frigid look at Blair and said, "Well, you didn't waste much time."

"It's not what you think," Blair said.

"She is just a child." Delia's tone was thick with indignation. "You should be ashamed of yourself. Anyway —" She got to her feet and headed toward Blair, waxy arms outstretched. "It's good to see you."

Blair hugged her. "You've got to eat something," she said automatically. Delia had lost more weight. She felt as brittle as a twig. "How are the T-cells holding?"

"I'm doing okay at the moment. I got searched at the airport."

"What?"

"I guess I look like a junkie with AIDS," Delia said wryly.

Blair didn't know what to say. She thought that after four years she'd come to terms with Delia's HIV-positive status. But she was consumed anew with panic. It was as though Delia was disappearing right before her — the absence of each pound more tangible as there was less and less to lose.

A guilty embarrassment plucked at her conscience. How could she be consumed with relationship dramas when her closest friend was fighting AIDS? How could she be so well in the face of Delia's fragility?

"Don't look at me like that," Delia said dryly. "I'm not dead yet. In fact, all I've had this year is a bout of pneumonia."

"Sorry." Blair dropped a kiss on her cheek. "How about brunch? Cassie sleeps during the day. She works night-shift."

"Really? Where does she work?"

Blair smoothed a clump of hair sticking up on the back of her head. "Let's talk over coffee."

"You're having me on." Delia stirred her vegetable juice. "An escort service?"

"She was desperate to send money home," Blair said.

"She doesn't —"

"She's the receptionist," Blair said sharply.

"Little Cassie . . ." Delia sighed. "I used to bounce that child on my knee."

Feeling uneasy, Blair ordered another coffee. "She's nearly twenty, Delia."

"So. What's the story? Is it all on, then?"

"Not exactly," Blair said. "We have an open-ended arrangement." Delia would relate to that, she felt certain. The woman had welcomed her husband's male lover into their household, after all.

Delia picked at her muffin. "You're talking nonmonogamous bliss?"

"Well, Cassie's very young," Blair began.

"And you're scared she'll dump you as soon as she finds her feet? Or was that her clitoris?"

Blair stared into the murky grounds in the bottom of her coffee cup. "I hate that you know me so well."

Delia gave a brief pained laugh. "Life's too short for bullshit, Blair. How do you really feel about her?"

"If you must know — pretty hot and bothered." Blair could almost feel Cassie kissing her sweetly.

"Then you know what I'd do if I were you?"

"What?"

"I'd grab her. I'd take the risk. You could be eaten by piranhas next week, and what would they write on your headstone? *At least she didn't get involved with a twenty-year-old.* Cold comfort, I'd say."

Blair took her thin hand. "You're a bad influence, Delia Grace."

"But I'm a good friend."

I'll miss you, Blair thought, feeling her eyes flood. Conscious she was squeezing Delia's hand too hard, she opened her fingers.

"Let's take a walk," Delia said, standing up. "I haven't seen the Botanic Gardens in years."

"Done." Blair paid the check.

As they left the café, she heard a diner remark, gazing at Delia, "Anorexic. How dreadful."

Cassie was still sleeping when they returned to the apartment.

"I have to lie down awhile," Delia said. "I'm exhausted." She opened her cabin bag and extracted various prescription bottles, tapping out pills into one hand.

"Is there anything I can get you?"

"No. I just need to sleep." Delia gave Blair a small hug. "Thanks for taking me to the gardens."

"I'm glad you're here," Blair said.

"I thought it was time."

Delia hadn't told Faith yet. She had asked Blair to drive her out to Narrung as soon as she'd recovered from her flight.

Blair filled a tall glass with ice and Bisleri water, the local equivalent of Perrier. Sitting at the dining table, she leafed through her notes on the documentary and knew for certain that she was not going to film it. Dean Wiebusch had called her yesterday, backing down from his previous stance. She had set a time to meet with him, but there seemed little point now.

Blair gazed out into the cloudless day, catching the sound of distant sirens. On the street below a couple of dogs were having a stand-off, watched by rows of pigeons perched along the sills of the building opposite. High above, a peregrine falcon wheeled, titillated by the presence of its preferred prey.

Impulsively Blair dialed Narrung's number.

"I thought you'd call." Faith sounded pleased.

Wondering how much Delia had told her, Blair said cautiously, "It looks like I'll be seeing you again very soon."

"Delia asked you about driving out?"

"I thought we could wait until the weekend so that Cassie could come," Blair said.

"Wonderful." Faith did not sound at all perturbed. "If it's any trouble Delia can take a bus to Bendigo and I'll pick her up."

"It's no trouble at all. I'm looking forward to it."

Blair knew she was speaking in banalities to avoid real conversation, but she didn't know what else to say. It was not her place to discuss either Cassie or Delia.

Faith must have read something into her silence, for she asked, "Is everything okay?"

Blair cleared her throat. "I've decided not to do my documentary."

"Does that mean you're going back home?"

"No." Blair was surprised at the immediacy of her response. "I'd like to stay here for a while."

"What are you going to do?"

"To be honest, I have no idea."

There was a brief silence. "Perhaps you could take a holiday," Faith suggested in a matter-of-fact tone.

"Perhaps I could manage Narrung while you did that."

Faith laughed. "Watch out. I might take you up on that offer."

"I hope you do," Blair said.

After they'd hung up, she finished her iced water then headed for the bedroom. Cassie was still asleep, cheeks flushed, mouth curved in the ghost of a smile.

Blair took off her shoes and lowered herself carefully onto the bed. Inhaling the scent of the sleeping woman, she closed her eyes and allowed herself to feel smugly content. She, Blair Carroll, discarded by her lover, was lying here next to a gorgeous young woman who wanted a relationship with her. It was a little scary, but very good for the ego.

CHAPTER SEVENTEEN

"I'm going by Southbank to see Marla," Blair said a few hours later, as Cassie stood by the open bedroom window combing tangles from her hair. "Do you want to come?"

Cassie cast a look in the direction of the spare room. "I don't know. Maybe Aunt Delia will wake up soon."

"I doubt it," Blair said. "She's taken two long flights in two days. She'll sleep for hours."

Yelping as her comb got stuck, Cassie grumbled, "I should get my head shaved."

Shuddering at the idea, Blair prompted, "Marla?"

Cassie gave a small evasive shrug. "Why do you have to see her anyway? I thought she was going back to Sydney."

Give me strength, Blair thought. She could almost see Cassie's interior reasoning process at work. Marla was attractive, by magazine standards anyway. And Blair was a lesbian. Marla was soon to leave town, and Blair was in the market for sex without commitment. It was a fling in the making. "Cassie," Blair said softly. "I'm not interested in Marla. She's not my type. Even if she were, there is the small matter of her heterosexuality."

"That doesn't seem to stop her flirting with you," Cassie said bluntly.

"Well, it stops me flirting with her."

Cassie put her comb away and made a show of buckling on a pair of sandals. "Okay. I'm ready," she announced in a subdued voice.

Detecting a hint of apology, Blair kept her tone very even. "Does this mean you're going to be civil to Marla?"

"You sound like my mother," Cassie accused.

Blair smiled. "I take that as a compliment."

Cassie had expected Marla to be glad to see Blair, but she was surprised to find herself included in the welcoming hugs.

Wafting a perfume that seemed too heavy for her, Marla led them into a spacious sitting room with French doors opening onto a balcony. "Do sit down. I've just made tea. Would you care for some?"

Perhaps she wasn't Blair's type, after all, Cassie mused. She was thin, and Blair said she preferred a woman with a solid body. Her legs were shaved, her nails were painted pale pink and her breasts were small. Clad in a pale yellow linen skirt and a sleeveless top in the same yellow with a thin cream stripe, she personified cool English elegance. Cassie could imagine her looking exactly the same when she was fifty.

"Cassie?" Marla held the teapot slightly aloft.

"Oh. No, thanks."

"There's juice in the fridge, if you'd rather," Marla said. "Just help yourself."

She didn't intend to sound patronizing, Cassie concluded. She was just being polite. Amused, she watched Blair accept the cup of tea Marla offered. Blair didn't like tea, but they'd discovered at Narrung that Marla made awful coffee.

"I took your advice," Marla said to Blair. "You're quite right. I can't keep running away. I called Mother and, wonderful news, she and Father have bought a cottage in Sussex. It sounds just perfect. I can probably get some locum work around the district, and I'll be safe for a while, especially if he thinks I'm still over here."

"That will give you time to see a lawyer," Blair said.

"Precisely." Marla lowered a thin slice of lemon into her tea. "Mother has located a chap who specializes in stalking cases. I'll see him as soon as I get back."

Marla's body language had changed since the weekend at Narrung, Cassie noticed. Her shoulders seemed looser, her face more animated.

"I really don't know how to thank you both." Marla's smile included Cassie. "I've felt so isolated and frightened."

"That's how he wants you to feel," Blair said. "It's a power trip for him."

"Sometimes, I wish I could kill him," Marla said quietly. "But I'd go to prison, of course. Ironic isn't it? They call it a justice system."

"Aunt Delia says the law is nothing but a set of rules lawyers designed to keep themselves in business," Cassie said.

Marla laughed. "I'm sure she has a point."

"And speaking of Delia." Blair abandoned her tea with a look of relief. "We should get home. Will you be okay?"

"Here, in the lap of luxury? — security, room service, neighbors who look like soap opera starlets . . ." Marla walked them to the door. "I'm sure I'll survive."

As they exited the building, a toothy young woman wearing pink lycra bike shorts and a Channel Seven singlet, bounced up the steps toward them. She seemed vaguely familiar.

"You know her?" Blair caught Cassie staring after her.

"Oh my God." Cassie gushed in phoney adoration. "That's Cissy Walters from *Home and Away*. She's in the same building. Maybe you'll get to meet her."

Blair gave her a long hard look. "I can hardly wait."

* * * * *

"Did you make up with her?" Nan asked as soon as Cassie got into work that evening.

"You could say that." Giving Jude a wave, Cassie perched on the arm of the sofa.

"I hear she's very yummy," Jude's mild brown eyes were teasing. "Obviously possessive."

Nan disagreed. "Controlling, more like it. You should watch that, Cassie," she advised. "She's a lot older than you. She probably expects you to run around after her and do exactly what she says."

On reflection that didn't sound so bad, Cassie thought. But she said, "Normally she isn't like that. I think she just got a shock when she found out about Beauties."

"So, are you permitted to keep working in this house of ill repute?" Jude inquired.

"Actually, she's offered me a job as her assistant," Cassie said.

"Making films?" Nan snatched up a ringing phone, said, "You too, asshole," and promptly hung up again.

"She needs an assistant." Cassie was aware she sounded defensive. Blair had explained that there was terrific career potential in the film and television industry. By working on a couple of projects, Cassie could find out if the field appealed to her.

Jude was clearly dubious. "Isn't that kind of manipulative? She doesn't want you working here, so she dreams up some job for you. You'd end up completely dependent on her. Is that what you want?"

"Of course not." Niggled by Jude's skepticism,

Cassie said stiffly, "Blair doesn't want to own me. She doesn't even want a relationship."

Nan snorted. "Did she tell you that?"

"She broke up with her lover recently," Cassie explained. "They were together for twenty years. She's —"

Nan burst out laughing. "Baby, she's got it bad for you. Take it from Aunty Nan. She's got it so bad she was almost crying when I let her in here. You should have seen it." She glanced at Jude, who waved her into silence as she took a call.

"She says she doesn't want to get serious," Cassie hissed.

Nan dragged her out into the lobby. "Listen to me, Cassie Jensen. She's as serious as they get, trust me. If you want her, all you have to do is reel her in."

"Don't let her emotionally blackmail you about the job." Jude appeared in the office doorway. "It's your life. You don't have to explain your choices to anybody."

"But I can't keep lying about what I do." Cassie said.

"You don't have to," Nan responded. "You can just let people believe what they want to believe."

"Most of our friends think we're telephone counselors," Jude said.

Cassie tried to imagine a life where you had to conceal who you were from the people closest to you. After just a few weeks of hiding the truth about her job from her mother and Blair, she felt like a nervous wreck.

"Doesn't it feel weird pretending all the time?" she asked Jude.

"I guess we've had plenty of practice from being in the closet," Jude said dryly. "My family had no idea about us until last Christmas."

Cassie was stunned. "But you and Nan have been together for ages."

"My parents still don't know," Nan put in. "And they're not likely to find out. I haven't seen them in ten years."

"We only told my parents because we're planning a baby," Jude said.

Nan planted a loud kiss on her lover's cheek. "That's why she was off work on Tuesday — morning sickness."

Cassie tried to stop herself from looking at Jude's stomach, but not in time.

"There's nothing to see just yet," Jude said. "But give me another six months . . ." She seemed tickled at Cassie's bemused silence, adding, "No, it's not an immaculate conception. We're having the turkey baster framed for the family album."

* * * * *

"She sleeps a lot," Cassie said, as Blair fixed breakfast the next day.

"The drugs have quite bad side effects," Blair explained.

Cassie chewed on her knuckles. "Why has she lost so much weight? Is that because of the drugs, too?"

"Maybe. It's also to do with her metabolism. The

virus has affected her immune system, so her body has to work extra hard to fight off infections. Here —" She handed Cassie a pitcher of orange juice.

Pouring it into tumblers, Cassie said, "What about Uncle Martin? Has he got it, too?"

"He's HIV-positive."

"So she caught it from him?" Cassie's voice rose slightly at this monstrous possibility.

"Maybe. They're not sure about that." According to Delia, she and Martin had been practicing safe sex since the late eighties. Her travels in Asia had exposed her to risk, she said. She had been injected with antibiotics in a Bombay clinic and was convinced the needles were not sterile.

Cassie was leaning against the window frame, her arms wrapped around her middle. Since the previous morning, when Delia had told her, Cassie had been very quiet. She'd asked Blair a few nervous questions about how the virus was transmitted, uncertain whether she was supposed to isolate her aunt's cutlery and bedding, or if sneezing was a risk. She knew about body fluids, she said. They had a cupboard full of condoms, latex gloves and oral dams at Beauties, and Nan and Jude had told her about sexually transmitted diseases.

Blair flipped the last pancake onto the stack and placed these on the table with a flask of maple syrup. Then she went to Cassie. "It's okay, honey," she said, stroking her hair. "I know how hard it is."

Cassie turned, her face stranded between sorrow and disbelief. "It's just not fair. She's too young." She clung to Blair, sobbing with childlike abandonment.

Making comforting sounds, Blair held her until the sobs subsided.

"It makes me think about Dad, too." Cassie drew back. "And Mom."

"I've been thinking about your mom, too," Blair said. "I have an idea I'd like to talk over with you."

Wiping her face on her sleeve, Cassie moved purposefully toward the table. "I'll pour the coffee, then."

She sounded so matter-of-fact, Blair was startled. Obviously, in coping with her father's death, Cassie had developed certain ways of dealing with grief. Blair was struck by her strength. She would be a formidable woman one day.

"So, what's your idea?" Cassie asked.

"It's about Narrung. I'd like to buy into the farm." All over the world, animal sanctuaries were participating in breeding programs, she explained. Their aim was to restock populations that had been reduced by habitat destruction. Narrung could operate such a program.

Cassie frowned. "You mean convert the farm into a zoo?"

"Not exactly. More of a sanctuary. We'd have to be open to visitors, for the revenue. But —"

"Open Narrung up for strangers!" Cassie groaned. "Imagine the litter problem."

"We're not talking about a theme park," Blair said.

Cassie played with her food. "When you say buy into the farm, what exactly do you mean?"

Sensing her unease, Blair said carefully, "It's like buying shares. I would buy part ownership from your mom, and the money I pay would be put towards converting the farm to a sanctuary. I know people all over the world who could help us."

"Have you talked about this with mom?" Cassie asked.

"I thought I'd discuss it with you first." This was the right answer, Blair thought, noting with relief the satisfaction that flickered across Cassie's features.

In silence, Cassie consumed her pancake. "It's a good idea," she said finally. "Why do you want to do it?"

"Lot's of reasons." Blair had gone over them a thousand times in her head, but it was impossible to explain everything — that she felt more and more like a ship at sea, that the end of her relationship, and Delia's illness, had severed her strongest ties to New York. "I think I've needed to change direction for a while now," she said. "This feels like the opportunity I've been waiting for."

"Do you really think it will work?" A hint of excitement entered Cassie's voice.

Blair took her hand. "I'm willing to bet my life savings on it."

CHAPTER EIGHTEEN

Installed in a makeshift bed in the back seat of the Land Cruiser, Delia slept most of the way to Narrung, Cassie throwing occasional agitated glances toward her.

Blair cast a quick look at Cassie's averted profile. Tears streaked her face. In her lap, her hands were neatly folded. Reaching across, Blair took one of them and brought it to her own lap, absently caressing it.

"It makes you think about life, doesn't it?" Cassie said very quietly.

Blair said nothing, overcome by a rush of

emotion. Things seemed so simple all of a sudden. She was here, driving in a strange land with the two people she cared about most in the world. The road stretched endlessly ahead, unshadowed beneath a sky as blue as a broken heart. The past seemed to recede with every mile they drove.

She held Cassie's hand more tightly, anchoring herself in a present that felt precious and real. "I love you, Cassie," she said.

Cassie's fingers laced between hers. "I love you too."

That evening all four women sat on the veranda at Narrung until well after midnight. Faith had spent the afternoon talking alone with her sister — making up for lost time, Blair supposed. She and Cassie had done pretty much the same.

"I'd forgotten how beautiful it is," Delia said. "It's so silent. Like a huge empty room with stars on the ceiling."

"Not many tonight," Faith commented, looking upward.

"What are we going to do?" Cassie said, as though everyone would know exactly what she was referring to.

Faith laughed. "About what, darling?"

"About this." Cassie waved an all encompassing hand. "About everything. How can we just sit here as if it's all okay?" Abruptly she got to her feet and ran out onto the lawn.

Blair moved to follow, but Faith arrested her with a gentle hand. "She's okay. Just letting off steam."

Silhouetted in the light from the veranda, Cassie turned a couple of cartwheels.

"God, it's hot," Delia said. "I can hardly breathe."

"I have an idea, Faith," Blair said. "About Narrung. I wondered if you might let me buy into the property."

Faith turned slowly, her expression contained.

"I have some capital," Blair found herself babbling. "I thought we could use it to make improvements. This place would be perfect for a wildlife park . . . a breeding sanctuary. We could extend your water system out beyond the house and set up a small research station. There are programs we could participate in . . . you can get funding . . ."

"Have you lost your mind?" Delia stared at her.

"It's not a crazy idea," Blair protested. "I've given it a lot of thought."

"Who would run this . . . sanctuary?" Faith asked. There was no mistaking the tinge of excitement in her voice.

"We would," Blair said. "You, me and Cassie."

"You'd live here? In the middle of nowhere." Delia was incredulous.

Faith tossed a cushion at her sister. "You're serious about this?" she asked Blair.

"I'm more serious than I've ever been in my life," Blair said. "I want a change." And I want your Cassie, she added mentally.

"I don't know what to say." Faith gave an odd-sounding laugh, then broke off at the sound of a sharp cry.

From the lawn Cassie was yelling unintelligibly, arms waving above her head. Blair leapt to her feet, imagining broken glass or snakebites.

Both she and Faith reached Cassie at the same time, Faith crying, "What! What's wrong?"

"Feel it!" Cassie shrieked, pointing up at the sky.

Blair stared up. Something wet hit her cheek. She was aware of Faith clutching her arm, shaking violently. Coming toward them Delia started to laugh, and quite suddenly they were all throwing off their clothes.

This is mad, Blair thought as she turned her face to the huge wet droplets. Reaching for Cassie, she pulled her close as a sheet of lightening threw their world into ghostly monochrome. "I love you," she murmured.

Cassie was less discreet. "Did you hear that?" she demanded of their small bedraggled gathering. "She loves me."

Faith patted her daughter. "I can tell." Catching Blair's swift glance, she added, "I knew it from the moment I saw her."

A few of the publications of
THE NAIAD PRESS, INC.
P.O. Box 10543 • Tallahassee, Florida 32302
Phone (904) 539-5965
Toll-Free Order Number: 1-800-533-1973
Mail orders welcome. Please include 15% postage.
Write or call for our free catalog which also features an
incredible selection of lesbian videos.

INNER CIRCLE by Claire McNab. 208 pp. 8th Carol Ashton
Mystery.   ISBN 1-56280-135-X $10.95

LESBIAN SEX: AN ORAL HISTORY by Susan Johnson.
240 pp. Need we say more?   ISBN 1-56280-142-2   14.95

BABY, IT'S COLD by Jaye Maiman. 256 pp. 5th Robin Miller
Mystery.   ISBN 1-56280-141-4   19.95

WILD THINGS by Karin Kallmaker. 240 pp. By the undisputed
mistress of lesbian romance.   ISBN 1-56280-139-2   10.95

THE GIRL NEXT DOOR by Mindy Kaplan. 208 pp. Just what
you'd expect.   ISBN 1-56280-140-6   10.95

NOW AND THEN by Penny Hayes. 240 pp. Romance on the
westward journey.   ISBN 1-56280-121-X   10.95

HEART ON FIRE by Diana Simmonds. 176 pp. The romantic and
erotic rival of *Curious Wine.*   ISBN 1-56280-152-X   10.95

DEATH AT LAVENDER BAY by Lauren Wright Douglas. 208 pp.
1st Allison O'Neil Mystery.   ISBN 1-56280-085-X   10.95

YES I SAID YES I WILL by Judith McDaniel. 272 pp. Hot
romance by famous author.   ISBN 1-56280-138-4   10.95

FORBIDDEN FIRES by Margaret C. Anderson. Edited by Mathilda
Hills. 176 pp. Famous author's "unpublished" Lesbian romance.
                                            ISBN 1-56280-123-6   21.95

SIDE TRACKS by Teresa Stores. 160 pp. Gender-bending
Lesbians on the road.   ISBN 1-56280-122-8   10.95

HOODED MURDER by Annette Van Dyke. 176 pp. 1st Jessie
Batelle Mystery.   ISBN 1-56280-134-1   10.95

WILDWOOD FLOWERS by Julia Watts. 208 pp. Hilarious and
heart-warming tale of true love.   ISBN 1-56280-127-9   10.95

NEVER SAY NEVER by Linda Hill. 224 pp. Rule #1: Never get involved
with . . .   ISBN 1-56280-126-0   10.95

THE SEARCH by Melanie McAllester. 240 pp. Exciting top cop
Tenny Mendoza case.   ISBN 1-56280-150-3   10.95

THE WISH LIST by Saxon Bennett. 192 pp. Romance through
the years.   ISBN 1-56280-125-2   10.95

FIRST IMPRESSIONS by Kate Calloway. 208 pp. P.I. Cassidy
James' first case.   ISBN 1-56280-133-3   10.95

OUT OF THE NIGHT by Kris Bruyer. 192 pp. Spine-tingling
thriller.   ISBN 1-56280-120-1   10.95

NORTHERN BLUE by Tracey Richardson. 224 pp. Police recruits
Miki & Miranda — passion in the line of fire. ISBN 1-56280-118-X 10.95

LOVE'S HARVEST by Peggy J. Herring. 176 pp. by the author of
Once More With Feeling.   ISBN 1-56280-117-1   10.95

THE COLOR OF WINTER by Lisa Shapiro. 208 pp. Romantic
love beyond your wildest dreams.   ISBN 1-56280-116-3   10.95

FAMILY SECRETS by Laura DeHart Young. 208 pp. Enthralling
romance and suspense.   ISBN 1-56280-119-8   10.95

INLAND PASSAGE by Jane Rule. 288 pp. Tales exploring conven-
tional & unconventional relationships.   ISBN 0-930044-56-8   10.95

DOUBLE BLUFF by Claire McNab. 208 pp. 7th Carol Ashton
Mystery.   ISBN 1-56280-096-5   10.95

BAR GIRLS by Lauran Hoffman. 176 pp. See the movie, read
the book!   ISBN 1-56280-115-5   10.95

THE FIRST TIME EVER edited by Barbara Grier & Christine
Cassidy. 272 pp. Love stories by Naiad Press authors.
                                            ISBN 1-56280-086-8   14.95

MISS PETTIBONE AND MISS McGRAW by Brenda Weathers.
208 pp. A charming ghostly love story.   ISBN 1-56280-151-1   10.95

CHANGES by Jackie Calhoun. 208 pp. Involved romance and
relationships.   ISBN 1-56280-083-3   10.95

FAIR PLAY by Rose Beecham. 256 pp. 3rd Amanda Valentine
Mystery.   ISBN 1-56280-081-7   10.95

PAXTON COURT by Diane Salvatore. 256 pp. Erotic and wickedly
funny contemporary tale about the business of learning to live
together.   ISBN 1-56280-109-0   21.95

PAYBACK by Celia Cohen. 176 pp. A gripping thriller of romance,
revenge and betrayal.   ISBN 1-56280-084-1   10.95

THE BEACH AFFAIR by Barbara Johnson. 224 pp. Sizzling
summer romance/mystery/intrigue.   ISBN 1-56280-090-6   10.95

GETTING THERE by Robbi Sommers. 192 pp. Nobody does it
like Robbi!   ISBN 1-56280-099-X   10.95

FINAL CUT by Lisa Haddock. 208 pp. 2nd Carmen Ramirez
Mystery.   ISBN 1-56280-088-4   10.95

FLASHPOINT by Katherine V. Forrest. 256 pp. A Lesbian
blockbuster! ISBN 1-56280-079-5 10.95

CLAIRE OF THE MOON by Nicole Conn. Audio Book —Read
by Marianne Hyatt. ISBN 1-56280-113-9 16.95

FOR LOVE AND FOR LIFE: INTIMATE PORTRAITS OF
LESBIAN COUPLES by Susan Johnson. 224 pp.
ISBN 1-56280-091-4 14.95

DEVOTION by Mindy Kaplan. 192 pp. See the movie — read
the book! ISBN 1-56280-093-0 10.95

SOMEONE TO WATCH by Jaye Maiman. 272 pp. 4th Robin
Miller Mystery. ISBN 1-56280-095-7 10.95

GREENER THAN GRASS by Jennifer Fulton. 208 pp. A young
woman — a stranger in her bed. ISBN 1-56280-092-2 10.95

TRAVELS WITH DIANA HUNTER by Regine Sands. Erotic
lesbian romp. Audio Book (2 cassettes) ISBN 1-56280-107-4 16.95

CABIN FEVER by Carol Schmidt. 256 pp. Sizzling suspense
and passion. ISBN 1-56280-089-1 10.95

THERE WILL BE NO GOODBYES by Laura DeHart Young. 192
pp. Romantic love, strength, and friendship. ISBN 1-56280-103-1 10.95

FAULTLINE by Sheila Ortiz Taylor. 144 pp. Joyous comic
lesbian novel. ISBN 1-56280-108-2 9.95

OPEN HOUSE by Pat Welch. 176 pp. 4th Helen Black Mystery.
ISBN 1-56280-102-3 10.95

ONCE MORE WITH FEELING by Peggy J. Herring. 240 pp.
Lighthearted, loving romantic adventure. ISBN 1-56280-089-2 10.95

FOREVER by Evelyn Kennedy. 224 pp. Passionate romance — love
overcoming all obstacles. ISBN 1-56280-094-9 10.95

WHISPERS by Kris Bruyer. 176 pp. Romantic ghost story
ISBN 1-56280-082-5 10.95

NIGHT SONGS by Penny Mickelbury. 224 pp. 2nd Gianna Maglione
Mystery. ISBN 1-56280-097-3 10.95

GETTING TO THE POINT by Teresa Stores. 256 pp. Classic
southern Lesbian novel. ISBN 1-56280-100-7 10.95

PAINTED MOON by Karin Kallmaker. 224 pp. Delicious
Kallmaker romance. ISBN 1-56280-075-2 10.95

THE MYSTERIOUS NAIAD edited by Katherine V. Forrest &
Barbara Grier. 320 pp. Love stories by Naiad Press authors.
ISBN 1-56280-074-4 14.95

DAUGHTERS OF A CORAL DAWN by Katherine V. Forrest.
240 pp. Tenth Anniversary Edition. ISBN 1-56280-104-X 10.95

BODY GUARD by Claire McNab. 208 pp. 6th Carol Ashton
Mystery. ISBN 1-56280-073-6 10.95

CACTUS LOVE by Lee Lynch. 192 pp. Stories by the beloved
storyteller.   ISBN 1-56280-071-X   9.95

SECOND GUESS by Rose Beecham. 216 pp. 2nd Amanda Valentine
Mystery.   ISBN 1-56280-069-8   9.95

THE SURE THING by Melissa Hartman. 208 pp. L.A. earthquake
romance.   ISBN 1-56280-078-7   9.95

A RAGE OF MAIDENS by Lauren Wright Douglas. 240 pp. 6th Caitlin
Reece Mystery.   ISBN 1-56280-068-X   10.95

TRIPLE EXPOSURE by Jackie Calhoun. 224 pp. Romantic drama
involving many characters.   ISBN 1-56280-067-1   10.95

UP, UP AND AWAY by Catherine Ennis. 192 pp. Delightful
romance.   ISBN 1-56280-065-5   9.95

PERSONAL ADS by Robbi Sommers. 176 pp. Sizzling short
stories.   ISBN 1-56280-059-0   10.95

FLASHPOINT by Katherine V. Forrest. 256 pp. Lesbian
blockbuster!   ISBN 1-56280-043-4   22.95

CROSSWORDS by Penny Sumner. 256 pp. 2nd Victoria Cross
Mystery.   ISBN 1-56280-064-7   9.95

SWEET CHERRY WINE by Carol Schmidt. 224 pp. A novel of
suspense.   ISBN 1-56280-063-9   9.95

CERTAIN SMILES by Dorothy Tell. 160 pp. Erotic short stories.
                                          ISBN 1-56280-066-3   9.95

EDITED OUT by Lisa Haddock. 224 pp. 1st Carmen Ramirez
Mystery.   ISBN 1-56280-077-9   9.95

WEDNESDAY NIGHTS by Camarin Grae. 288 pp. Sexy
adventure.   ISBN 1-56280-060-4   10.95

SMOKEY O by Celia Cohen. 176 pp. Relationships on the
playing field.   ISBN 1-56280-057-4   9.95

KATHLEEN O'DONALD by Penny Hayes. 256 pp. Rose and
Kathleen find each other and employment in 1909 NYC.
                                          ISBN 1-56280-070-1   9.95

STAYING HOME by Elisabeth Nonas. 256 pp. Molly and Alix
want a baby . . . or do they?   ISBN 1-56280-076-0   10.95

TRUE LOVE by Jennifer Fulton. 240 pp. Six lesbians searching
for love in all the "right" places.   ISBN 1-56280-035-3   10.95

GARDENIAS WHERE THERE ARE NONE by Molleen Zanger.
176 pp. Why is Melanie inextricably drawn to the old house?
                                          ISBN 1-56280-056-6   9.95

KEEPING SECRETS by Penny Mickelbury. 208 pp. 1st Gianna
Maglione Mystery.   ISBN 1-56280-052-3   9.95

THE ROMANTIC NAIAD edited by Katherine V. Forrest &
Barbara Grier. 336 pp. Love stories by Naiad Press authors.
ISBN 1-56280-054-X   14.95

UNDER MY SKIN by Jaye Maiman. 336 pp. 3rd Robin Miller
Mystery.   ISBN 1-56280-049-3.   10.95

CAR POOL by Karin Kallmaker. 272pp. Lesbians on wheels
and then some!   ISBN 1-56280-048-5   10.95

NOT TELLING MOTHER: STORIES FROM A LIFE by Diane
Salvatore. 176 pp. Her 3rd novel.   ISBN 1-56280-044-2   9.95

GOBLIN MARKET by Lauren Wright Douglas. 240pp. 5th Caitlin
Reece Mystery.   ISBN 1-56280-047-7   10.95

LONG GOODBYES by Nikki Baker. 256 pp. 3rd Virginia Kelly
Mystery.   ISBN 1-56280-042-6   9.95

FRIENDS AND LOVERS by Jackie Calhoun. 224 pp. Mid-
western Lesbian lives and loves.   ISBN 1-56280-041-8   10.95

THE CAT CAME BACK by Hilary Mullins. 208 pp. Highly
praised Lesbian novel.   ISBN 1-56280-040-X   9.95

BEHIND CLOSED DOORS by Robbi Sommers. 192 pp. Hot,
erotic short stories.   ISBN 1-56280-039-6   9.95

CLAIRE OF THE MOON by Nicole Conn. 192 pp. See the
movie — read the book!   ISBN 1-56280-038-8   10.95

SILENT HEART by Claire McNab. 192 pp. Exotic Lesbian
romance.   ISBN 1-56280-036-1   10.95

HAPPY ENDINGS by Kate Brandt. 272 pp. Intimate conversations
with Lesbian authors.   ISBN 1-56280-050-7   10.95

THE SPY IN QUESTION by Amanda Kyle Williams. 256 pp.
4th Madison McGuire Mystery.   ISBN 1-56280-037-X   9.95

SAVING GRACE by Jennifer Fulton. 240 pp. Adventure and
romantic entanglement.   ISBN 1-56280-051-5   10.95

THE YEAR SEVEN by Molleen Zanger. 208 pp. Women surviving
in a new world.   ISBN 1-56280-034-5   9.95

CURIOUS WINE by Katherine V. Forrest. 176 pp. Tenth Anniver-
sary Edition. The most popular contemporary Lesbian love story.
ISBN 1-56280-053-1   10.95
Audio Book (2 cassettes)   ISBN 1-56280-105-8   16.95

CHAUTAUQUA by Catherine Ennis. 192 pp. Exciting, romantic
adventure.   ISBN 1-56280-032-9   9.95

A PROPER BURIAL by Pat Welch. 192 pp. 3rd Helen Black
Mystery.   ISBN 1-56280-033-7   9.95

SILVERLAKE HEAT: A Novel of Suspense by Carol Schmidt.
240 pp. Rhonda is as hot as Laney's dreams.   ISBN 1-56280-031-0   9.95

LOVE, ZENA BETH by Diane Salvatore. 224 pp. The most talked
about lesbian novel of the nineties! ISBN 1-56280-030-2   10.95

A DOORYARD FULL OF FLOWERS by Isabel Miller. 160 pp.
Stories incl. 2 sequels to *Patience and Sarah.* ISBN 1-56280-029-9   9.95

MURDER BY TRADITION by Katherine V. Forrest. 288 pp. 4th
Kate Delafield Mystery. ISBN 1-56280-002-7   11.95

THE EROTIC NAIAD edited by Katherine V. Forrest & Barbara
Grier. 224 pp. Love stories by Naiad Press authors.
ISBN 1-56280-026-4   14.95

DEAD CERTAIN by Claire McNab. 224 pp. 5th Carol Ashton
Mystery. ISBN 1-56280-027-2   9.95

CRAZY FOR LOVING by Jaye Maiman. 320 pp. 2nd Robin Miller
Mystery. ISBN 1-56280-025-6   11.95

STONEHURST by Barbara Johnson. 176 pp. Passionate regency
romance. ISBN 1-56280-024-8   9.95

INTRODUCING AMANDA VALENTINE by Rose Beecham.
256 pp. 1st Amanda Valentine Mystery. ISBN 1-56280-021-3   10.95

UNCERTAIN COMPANIONS by Robbi Sommers. 204 pp.
Steamy, erotic novel. ISBN 1-56280-017-5   9.95

A TIGER'S HEART by Lauren W. Douglas. 240 pp. 4th Caitlin
Reece Mystery. ISBN 1-56280-018-3   9.95

PAPERBACK ROMANCE by Karin Kallmaker. 256 pp. A
delicious romance. ISBN 1-56280-019-1   10.95

MORTON RIVER VALLEY by Lee Lynch. 304 pp. Lee Lynch
at her best! ISBN 1-56280-016-7   9.95

THE LAVENDER HOUSE MURDER by Nikki Baker. 224 pp.
2nd Virginia Kelly Mystery. ISBN 1-56280-012-4   9.95

PASSION BAY by Jennifer Fulton. 224 pp. Passionate romance,
virgin beaches, tropical skies. ISBN 1-56280-028-0   10.95

STICKS AND STONES by Jackie Calhoun. 208 pp. Contemporary
lesbian lives and loves. ISBN 1-56280-020-5   9.95
Audio Book (2 cassettes) ISBN 1-56280-106-6   16.95

DELIA IRONFOOT by Jeane Harris. 192 pp. Adventure for Delia
and Beth in the Utah mountains. ISBN 1-56280-014-0   9.95

UNDER THE SOUTHERN CROSS by Claire McNab. 192 pp.
Romantic nights Down Under. ISBN 1-56280-011-6   9.95

GRASSY FLATS by Penny Hayes. 256 pp. Lesbian romance in
the '30s. ISBN 1-56280-010-8   9.95

A SINGULAR SPY by Amanda K. Williams. 192 pp. 3rd
Madison McGuire Mystery. ISBN 1-56280-008-6   8.95

THE END OF APRIL by Penny Sumner. 240 pp. 1st Victoria
Cross Mystery. ISBN 1-56280-007-8   8.95

HOUSTON TOWN by Deborah Powell. 208 pp. A Hollis
Carpenter Mystery.   ISBN 1-56280-006-X   8.95

KISS AND TELL by Robbi Sommers. 192 pp. Scorching stories
by the author of *Pleasures*.   ISBN 1-56280-005-1   10.95

STILL WATERS by Pat Welch. 208 pp. 2nd Helen Black Mystery.
                                      ISBN 0-941483-97-5   9.95

TO LOVE AGAIN by Evelyn Kennedy. 208 pp. Wildly romantic
love story.   ISBN 0-941483-85-1   9.95

IN THE GAME by Nikki Baker. 192 pp. 1st Virginia Kelly
Mystery.   ISBN 1-56280-004-3   9.95

AVALON by Mary Jane Jones. 256 pp. A Lesbian Arthurian
romance.   ISBN 0-941483-96-7   9.95

STRANDED by Camarin Grae. 320 pp. Entertaining, riveting
adventure.   ISBN 0-941483-99-1   9.95

THE DAUGHTERS OF ARTEMIS by Lauren Wright Douglas.
240 pp. 3rd Caitlin Reece Mystery.   ISBN 0-941483-95-9   9.95

CLEARWATER by Catherine Ennis. 176 pp. Romantic secrets
of a small Louisiana town.   ISBN 0-941483-65-7   8.95

THE HALLELUJAH MURDERS by Dorothy Tell. 176 pp. 2nd
Poppy Dillworth Mystery.   ISBN 0-941483-88-6   8.95

SECOND CHANCE by Jackie Calhoun. 256 pp. Contemporary
Lesbian lives and loves.   ISBN 0-941483-93-2   9.95

BENEDICTION by Diane Salvatore. 272 pp. Striking, contemporary romantic novel.   ISBN 0-941483-90-8   9.95

BLACK IRIS by Jeane Harris. 192 pp. Caroline's hidden past . . .
                                      ISBN 0-941483-68-1   8.95

TOUCHWOOD by Karin Kallmaker. 240 pp. Loving, May/
December romance.   ISBN 0-941483-76-2   9.95

COP OUT by Claire McNab. 208 pp. 4th Carol Ashton Mystery.
                                      ISBN 0-941483-84-3   10.95

THE BEVERLY MALIBU by Katherine V. Forrest. 288 pp. 3rd
Kate Delafield Mystery.   ISBN 0-941483-48-7   11.95

THAT OLD STUDEBAKER by Lee Lynch. 272 pp. Andy's affair
with Regina and her attachment to her beloved car.
                                      ISBN 0-941483-82-7   9.95

PASSION'S LEGACY by Lori Paige. 224 pp. Sarah is swept into
the arms of Augusta Pym in this delightful historical romance.
                                      ISBN 0-941483-81-9   8.95

THE PROVIDENCE FILE by Amanda Kyle Williams. 256 pp.
2nd Madison McGuire Mystery.   ISBN 0-941483-92-4   8.95

I LEFT MY HEART by Jaye Maiman. 320 pp. 1st Robin Miller
Mystery.   ISBN 0-941483-72-X   10.95

THE PRICE OF SALT by Patricia Highsmith (writing as Claire Morgan). 288 pp. Classic lesbian novel, first issued in 1952 . . . acknowledged by its author under her own, very famous, name.
ISBN 1-56280-003-5   9.95

SIDE BY SIDE by Isabel Miller. 256 pp. From beloved author of *Patience and Sarah.*   ISBN 0-941483-77-0   10.95

STAYING POWER: LONG TERM LESBIAN COUPLES by Susan E. Johnson. 352 pp. Joys of coupledom. ISBN 0-941-483-75-4   14.95

SLICK by Camarin Grae. 304 pp. Exotic, erotic adventure.
ISBN 0-941483-74-6   9.95

NINTH LIFE by Lauren Wright Douglas. 256 pp. 2nd Caitlin Reece Mystery.   ISBN 0-941483-50-9   8.95

PLAYERS by Robbi Sommers. 192 pp. Sizzling, erotic novel.
ISBN 0-941483-73-8   9.95

MURDER AT RED ROOK RANCH by Dorothy Tell. 224 pp. 1st Poppy Dillworth Mystery.   ISBN 0-941483-80-0   8.95

A ROOM FULL OF WOMEN by Elisabeth Nonas. 256 pp. Contemporary Lesbian lives.   ISBN 0-941483-69-X   9.95

THEME FOR DIVERSE INSTRUMENTS by Jane Rule. 208 pp. Powerful romantic lesbian stories.   ISBN 0-941483-63-0   8.95

CLUB 12 by Amanda Kyle Williams. 288 pp. Espionage thriller featuring a lesbian agent!   ISBN 0-941483-64-9   8.95

DEATH DOWN UNDER by Claire McNab. 240 pp. 3rd Carol Ashton Mystery.   ISBN 0-941483-39-8   9.95

MONTANA FEATHERS by Penny Hayes. 256 pp. Vivian and Elizabeth find love in frontier Montana.   ISBN 0-941483-61-4   8.95

LIFESTYLES by Jackie Calhoun. 224 pp. Contemporary Lesbian lives and loves.   ISBN 0-941483-57-6   10.95

WILDERNESS TREK by Dorothy Tell. 192 pp. Six women on vacation learning "new" skills.   ISBN 0-941483-60-6   8.95

MURDER BY THE BOOK by Pat Welch. 256 pp. 1st Helen Black Mystery.   ISBN 0-941483-59-2   9.95

THERE'S SOMETHING I'VE BEEN MEANING TO TELL YOU Ed. by Loralee MacPike. 288 pp. Gay men and lesbians coming out to their children.   ISBN 0-941483-44-4   9.95

LIFTING BELLY by Gertrude Stein. Ed. by Rebecca Mark. 104 pp. Erotic poetry.   ISBN 0-941483-51-7   10.95

AFTER THE FIRE by Jane Rule. 256 pp. Warm, human novel by this incomparable author.   ISBN 0-941483-45-2   8.95

PLEASURES by Robbi Sommers. 204 pp. Unprecedented eroticism.   ISBN 0-941483-49-5   8.95

EDGEWISE by Camarin Grae. 372 pp. Spellbinding
adventure.   ISBN 0-941483-19-3   9.95

FATAL REUNION by Claire McNab. 224 pp. 2nd Carol Ashton
Mystery.   ISBN 0-941483-40-1   10.95

IN EVERY PORT by Karin Kallmaker. 228 pp. Jessica's sexy,
adventuresome travels.   ISBN 0-941483-37-7   10.95

OF LOVE AND GLORY by Evelyn Kennedy. 192 pp. Exciting
WWII romance.   ISBN 0-941483-32-0   10.95

CLICKING STONES by Nancy Tyler Glenn. 288 pp. Love
transcending time.   ISBN 0-941483-31-2   9.95

SOUTH OF THE LINE by Catherine Ennis. 216 pp. Civil War
adventure.   ISBN 0-941483-29-0   8.95

WOMAN PLUS WOMAN by Dolores Klaich. 300 pp. Supurb
Lesbian overview.   ISBN 0-941483-28-2   9.95

THE FINER GRAIN by Denise Ohio. 216 pp. Brilliant young
college lesbian novel.   ISBN 0-941483-11-8   8.95

OCTOBER OBSESSION by Meredith More. Josie's rich, secret
Lesbian life.   ISBN 0-941483-18-5   8.95

BEFORE STONEWALL: THE MAKING OF A GAY AND
LESBIAN COMMUNITY by Andrea Weiss & Greta Schiller.
96 pp., 25 illus.   ISBN 0-941483-20-7   7.95

OSTEN'S BAY by Zenobia N. Vole. 204 pp. Sizzling adventure
romance set on Bonaire.   ISBN 0-941483-15-0   8.95

LESSONS IN MURDER by Claire McNab. 216 pp. 1st Carol Ashton
Mystery.   ISBN 0-941483-14-2   10.95

YELLOWTHROAT by Penny Hayes. 240 pp. Margarita, bandit,
kidnaps Julia.   ISBN 0-941483-10-X   8.95

SAPPHISTRY: THE BOOK OF LESBIAN SEXUALITY by
Pat Califia. 3d edition, revised. 208 pp.   ISBN 0-941483-24-X   10.95

CHERISHED LOVE by Evelyn Kennedy. 192 pp. Erotic Lesbian
love story.   ISBN 0-941483-08-8   10.95

THE SECRET IN THE BIRD by Camarin Grae. 312 pp. Striking,
psychological suspense novel.   ISBN 0-941483-05-3   8.95

TO THE LIGHTNING by Catherine Ennis. 208 pp. Romantic
Lesbian 'Robinson Crusoe' adventure.   ISBN 0-941483-06-1   8.95

DREAMS AND SWORDS by Katherine V. Forrest. 192 pp.
Romantic, erotic, imaginative stories.   ISBN 0-941483-03-7   10.95

MEMORY BOARD by Jane Rule. 336 pp. Memorable novel
about an aging Lesbian couple.   ISBN 0-941483-02-9   12.95

THE ALWAYS ANONYMOUS BEAST by Lauren Wright Douglas.
224 pp. 1st Caitlin Reece Mystery.
                                              ISBN 0-941483-04-5   8.95

THE BLACK AND WHITE OF IT by Ann Allen Shockley.
144 pp. Short stories.   ISBN 0-930044-96-7   7.95

SAY JESUS AND COME TO ME by Ann Allen Shockley. 288
pp. Contemporary romance.   ISBN 0-930044-98-3   8.95

MURDER AT THE NIGHTWOOD BAR by Katherine V. Forrest.
240 pp. 2nd Kate Delafield Mystery.   ISBN 0-930044-92-4   11.95

WINGED DANCER by Camarin Grae. 228 pp. Erotic Lesbian
adventure story.   ISBN 0-930044-88-6   8.95

PAZ by Camarin Grae. 336 pp. Romantic Lesbian adventurer
with the power to change the world.   ISBN 0-930044-89-4   8.95

SOUL SNATCHER by Camarin Grae. 224 pp. A puzzle, an
adventure, a mystery — Lesbian romance.   ISBN 0-930044-90-8   8.95

THE LOVE OF GOOD WOMEN by Isabel Miller. 224 pp.
Long-awaited new novel by the author of the beloved *Patience
and Sarah*.   ISBN 0-930044-81-9   8.95

THE HOUSE AT PELHAM FALLS by Brenda Weathers. 240
pp. Suspenseful Lesbian ghost story.   ISBN 0-930044-79-7   7.95

PEMBROKE PARK by Michelle Martin. 256 pp. Derring-do
and daring romance in Regency England. ISBN 0-930044-77-0   7.95

THE LONG TRAIL by Penny Hayes. 248 pp. Vivid adventures
of two women in love in the old west. ISBN 0-930044-76-2   8.95

AN EMERGENCE OF GREEN by Katherine V. Forrest. 288
pp. Powerful novel of sexual discovery.   ISBN 0-930044-69-X   11.95

THE LESBIAN PERIODICALS INDEX edited by Claire Potter.
432 pp. Author & subject index.   ISBN 0-930044-74-6   12.95

DESERT OF THE HEART by Jane Rule. 224 pp. A classic;
basis for the movie *Desert Hearts*.   ISBN 0-930044-73-8   10.95

TORCHLIGHT TO VALHALLA by Gale Wilhelm. 128 pp.
Classic novel by a great Lesbian writer. ISBN 0-930044-68-1   7.95

LESBIAN NUNS: BREAKING SILENCE edited by Rosemary
Curb and Nancy Manahan. 432 pp. Unprecedented autobiographies
of religious life.   ISBN 0-930044-62-2   9.95

SEX VARIANT WOMEN IN LITERATURE by Jeannette
Howard Foster. 448 pp. Literary history.   ISBN 0-930044-65-7   8.95

A HOT-EYED MODERATE by Jane Rule. 252 pp. Hard-hitting
essays on gay life; writing; art.   ISBN 0-930044-57-6   7.95

These are just a few of the many Naiad Press titles — we are the oldest and
largest lesbian/feminist publishing company in the world. We also offer an
enormous selection of lesbian video products. Please request a complete
catalog. We offer personal service; we encourage and welcome direct mail
orders from individuals who have limited access to bookstores carrying our
publications.